TWO
VICTIMS

Detective Rachel King Book 2

HELEN H. DURRANT

Published in paperback 2021
by Joffe Books, London
www.joffebooks.com

First published in Great Britain in 2019

ISBN: 978-1-78931-631-5

Printed and bound by CPI Group (UK) Ltd, Croydon, CR0 4YY

For all the reviewers and bloggers who add so much to a book's success. And a very special thank-you to Jill who arranges the blog tours, and puts on such fab launch parties.

PROLOGUE

The tuneless whistling grew louder. Stomach lurching, Ruby shrank back against the wall. He was coming for her. *Think! You can't muck this up. It could be the only chance you get.*

She'd been locked in this cold, dark room for hours. But dark and cold were nothing compared to what was coming. Fear seized her by the throat. She was weak. Her half-starved body wouldn't stand many more of the beatings he meted out.

Ruby knew her mistake — she'd trusted the wrong man. Not only that, she'd asked too many questions and turned herself into a liability, a weak link in an otherwise robust chain. Vasile liked her, and she'd used that to try and persuade him to help her get free. He'd talked about leaving the UK, going back home, and had eventually agreed to take her with him. But he'd made a mistake. A few nights ago when he'd been drunk, Ruby had got her hands on his mobile, seen his contacts and worked things out. Now she knew the truth, and that made her a burden. Knowing who was controlling this enterprise was as good as a death sentence.

Trapped in this place, Ruby realised too late that she couldn't trust anyone, and particularly not Vasile. In an effort to save his own skin, he'd told Nicu to warn the boss.

Nicu was charged with keeping the girls under control. He lost it, flew at her in a rage and finished by locking her up.

Ruby was sure he would kill her. Girls had gone missing in the past, what difference would one more make?

A shaft of light pierced the dark room, and Ruby screwed up her eyes against the glare.

"Move!" A gruff male voice called from the doorway.

Not Nicu this time, but a stranger. "Where're you taking me?" she asked.

He grabbed her arm, pulling her towards him. "You're a pretty one, aren't you? We wouldn't want to spoil that." He accompanied this threat with an evil smile.

Ruby recoiled. He'd brought her to within inches of his face. He hadn't shaved and his rotting teeth stank to high heaven.

"Please, let me go. I'll keep quiet and disappear. You'll never hear from me again, I promise."

That made him laugh. "Once we're outside, you don't talk to anyone. Understand?"

He pushed her in front of him along a dingy hallway. Moments later, Ruby felt the cold night air prickle her skin. She could see street lights and cars parked alongside the kerb.

The man stopped, loosening his grip for a moment, and felt around in his jacket pocket. He'd been distracted by the beep of his mobile.

This was her chance.

Ruby kicked out, tore her arm from his grasp and ran. She'd no idea where she was going and what was at the end of the street. Her only thought was to find someone to help her.

Within seconds, a car pulled up alongside her. "Problem, lass?" the driver called out.

Gasping for breath, Ruby could barely get the words out. "I . . . I'm being kept . . . prisoner. Back there. A man . . ."

The passenger door swung open. "Get in."

Ruby flopped onto the seat and slid down out of sight. "I can't thank you enough. I thought he'd kill me."

The driver turned and smiled at her. "He might yet. No one likes a girl who doesn't know her place. Those who give me trouble are always punished. Wasn't today warning enough?"

Nicu! She gaped in horror. She'd made a terrible mistake. She hadn't recognised him in the dark and with those shades on.

"There's a pile of clothes on the back seat. Get them on. Keep your mouth shut and do what I tell you. Cross me again and I'll tell the boss what you know. I do that, and you're dead." He dumped a large make-up bag on her lap. "You're going out tonight. Behave, please the punters, and you might get a bed to sleep in later."

CHAPTER ONE

Day One

Carrying a heavy tray of food, DCI Rachel King picked her way carefully between the packed tables. It was teatime, and the café was busy with shoppers. The Trafford Centre was the last place Rachel wanted to be, but she'd promised her fourteen-year-old daughter Mia a treat. They'd been to parents' evening at the school, and Mia had done well.

"Burgers and coke. Big deal! Ella's mum's taking her to that swanky new place in Spinning Fields."

"What about the clothes, then?" Rachel said, somewhat annoyed. "Don't forget them. That dress alone cost a bomb, you know."

Mia grabbed her burger. "You'd have bought me something new anyway. It's the school disco in a couple of weeks."

"Don't count on it. You've got a wardrobe full of stuff. You're such a diva." Rachel grinned. It was good to see the girl cheerful. She'd had a difficult couple of months. In the course of a particularly nasty murder case, Mia had been kidnapped. The experience had left its mark. For a while, she'd been scared of her own shadow.

"Your mobile's ringing." Mia nodded at the phone lying on the table. "Ignore it. It's bound to be work. Go on, I dare you. Let them wait for once."

Rachel shook her head. "You know I can't do that." She peered at the name on the screen — Elwyn Pryce, her sergeant. He wouldn't ring unless he had to. It must be something urgent.

"I know you're off tonight, ma'am," he said, "but we've got a situation."

Rachel could hear voices and traffic in the background. "What's up?"

"We've got a body, a woman. Only been dead a couple of hours, Butterfield reckons."

Dr Colin Butterfield was the pathologist. "Where are you?" she asked.

"Beswick. Just off Ashton Old Road — that new building site near the supermarket."

"I'm at the Trafford Centre with Mia. What with the motorway traffic at this hour, I might be a while. Hold the fort, Elwyn. I'll have to drop Mia off at the station first. Make sure the site is kept secure."

Mia wasn't happy. "I don't want dropping anywhere. Why can't I go home?"

"It won't be for long." Rachel promised the sullen girl. "You can sit in my office and Facetime Ella, show her your dress." Rachel smiled. "You can ring Meggy too while you're at it, tell her what's happened."

Megan was her eldest daughter, eighteen now and a student at Manchester Metropolitan University.

"Meggy's out tonight. She's gone to some party in town."

Rachel frowned. She didn't remember Megan saying anything about a party. "Boy involved, is there?"

Mia shrugged. "If there is, she didn't say anything to me."

"Eat up," Rachel urged, gulping down her coffee. "You can bring the drink with you."

* * *

5

By the time Rachel arrived at the scene, dusk had fallen. Lighting had been erected, illuminating the desolate patch of ground and the body, now covered with a tarpaulin.

"She's in that trench over there," DS Elwyn Pryce said.

She and the softly-spoken Welshman had worked together for a while now and had formed a successful partnership. Rachel trusted Elwyn and valued his judgement. He wasn't much older than she was, and not bad looking. Colleagues often thought there was more than just work going on between them, but they were wrong. Rachel saw Elwyn as a friend and teammate, nothing else.

She looked around her at the tract of open land, punctuated by a criss-cross of trenches.

"They're ready for filling with concrete tomorrow." A man spoke from somewhere behind her. "Once it's set, we'll have the foundations for those houses we're building."

Rachel turned towards him. "And you are?"

"Fred Turner — site manager." He smiled at her.

"Seems she was found just in time. Does it look like whoever did it made any attempt to hide her?" Rachel asked Elwyn.

"They tipped a bag of sand over her." This new voice belonged to a woman, invisible in the shadow beyond the circle of light. "Not a particularly good job either. Done in haste, I'd say. It's been raining, so most of it washed away. Hence she was spotted by Mr Turner here."

"Jude!" Rachel exclaimed. "Great to have you back."

Judith Glover was a senior forensic investigator who worked with Dr Jason Fox. Despite a ten year age difference, she was an old friend of Rachel's.

"Miss me?"

"Of course, though Jason did his best." Rachel smiled at the figure emerging from the dark.

"I imagine he did, but he hasn't got my touch, has he?" Jude quipped.

"Are you sure you should be scrambling around on your knees like that? What about your injuries?" Rachel asked.

"I was lucky, I had a brilliant surgeon. The operation was successful, and now my leg's as good as new."

Six months ago, while on a case, Jude had fallen through the roof of a warehouse. She'd broken her leg badly and had been out of commission ever since. Rachel had truly missed her. Jude was excellent at her job and was often able to offer vital insights into how a crime had been committed.

"How long has she been dead?" Rachel asked Butterfield.

"Less than an hour," was his measured reply.

Rachel checked her watch. That would put the time of death at about eight that evening.

"They certainly had no finesse," Jude said. "Whoever did this simply put a bullet in her skull. We found her in the trench at the place where she fell."

"Seen enough, DCI King? Can we take her now?" Butterfield said.

"Fine with me," Jude said, and looked at Rachel, who nodded.

"PM?" she asked.

"In the morning. I'll start at ten," Butterfield replied.

The mortuary technicians carefully lifted the body and laid it on a stretcher.

Once she was out, Rachel and Jude knelt down and took a close look at where she'd been.

"There's a lot of blood in the trench." Jude was painstakingly scraping away the sand and taking samples. "I think she was shot and lay here for a short while before she died. Hence the blood."

"Did she die from the bullet wound or did the sand suffocate her?"

"The PM will determine that," Jude said.

"Any of her belongings found?" Rachel asked.

"Not so far. No bag, and no coat or jacket either. From what I saw, she was wearing a skirt, a jumper and underwear."

"No shoes?"

"Nope." Jude shook her head.

"Rachel!" Elwyn called. "There's CCTV at all the entrances. Mr Turner's sorting it for me."

That was something at least. Rachel smiled at Jude. "If we're lucky, we might get a car registration number."

But Jude wasn't listening. She appeared to be concentrating hard on a patch a few feet further up the trench, brushing away the mingled sand and earth.

Rachel leaned forward to take a closer look. "Found something?"

"I'm afraid so. There's something else here."

"Will it help identify her?"

Jude met Rachel's eyes. She shook her head. "I doubt it. I'm afraid we have a second body. Digging this trench probably disturbed it. And this one's been here a bit longer."

CHAPTER TWO

Day Two

"You left me stuck in your office for hours," Mia complained at breakfast the following morning. "I thought you were never coming to pick me up. What was so important?"

"As I told you last night, I can't discuss it, sweetie. Sorry," Rachel said.

"I was bored stiff. That policeman from downstairs kept talking to me about his granddaughter."

Rachel smiled to herself. "He was just keeping you company." She looked around. "Seen Meggy this morning?"

"She didn't come home. She said that might happen."

Rachel raised her eyes from that morning's post, mostly junk mail. "Do you know who she went out with?"

"I presume it was that new friend Shannon and some others. She didn't say much, just that she might not be back."

"Okay, I'll ring her in a bit. Had your shot yet?"

Mia nodded. She suffered from type 1 diabetes and took insulin by injection each day.

"It'll be your dad's for tea. I'll probably be late," Rachel said.

"Does he know? If he doesn't, will you square it with him?"

That was an odd thing to say. Alan King, their dad, only lived next door, and the girls usually came and went as they pleased. "He won't mind, he's working at home all day. He'll be pleased to see you."

"Don't think so," Mia said. "He's been a bit off with me recently. I must have done something wrong."

Mia went to get her stuff for school, leaving Rachel at the kitchen table, quietly seething. She had a shrewd idea of what this was about. She picked up her mobile and rang him.

"Mia's with you later," she told him firmly. "I'll be late. You okay with that?"

"Yes, I suppose so. Will she have to stay overnight?"

"I don't know, Alan. What difference does it make? She has her own room at yours, for God's sake."

"We need to talk, Rachel, clear the air."

"Whatever needs saying, Alan, don't you dare take it out on our Mia."

With those words, she cut him off. If he was acting up because of rumours he'd heard about Jed McAteer, if he made Mia feel awkward in any way, she'd damn well kill him!

She was getting all het up, and that wouldn't do, not today. Trust Alan to be like this just when she had a new case on her hands. She relied on him to look after Mia when she wasn't around, make sure she managed her injections and ate regularly. With all the demands of her job, Rachel needed him. She ran her fingers through her curly red hair and dragged it off her forehead. She kept meaning to get it cut, but she never seemed to find the time.

* * *

The team — DS Elwyn Pryce, DC Jonny Farrell and DC Amy Metcalfe —gathered in the main office. As usual, Jonny was stylish in a sharp suit, obviously tailor-made, a crisp white shirt and shiny shoes. God knows how he afforded it. Rachel had seen him in half a dozen different suits this month. Amy kept turning round to look at him, blonde hair swinging about her face. The pretty DC was flirting. This was not something to be encouraged in members of the same team. It caused too much hassle.

"Last night two bodies were discovered on a building site in Beswick. One was female and the other yet to be determined, although on first examination that one was thought to be female too. The more recent victim was shot through the head and dumped no more than two hours before the alarm was raised. No belongings were found, apart from what she was wearing, and her identity is unknown. The second one has been in the ground for some time, according to Dr Glover."

"Are the killings connected?" DC Amy Metcalfe asked.

"We've no idea," Rachel replied. "I'm hopeful that Dr Butterfield, the pathologist, will shed some light on the matter. The site manager is emailing over the CCTV. Amy, can you check all vehicles that entered and left the site last night? Get the registration numbers and we'll go from there."

"Do you want me to check missing persons, ma'am?" Amy asked.

"Yes, for the female killed last night, but until we have a time frame for the other one, you can leave it for now."

Rachel turned to Jonny. "I want to know who owns that site, also what was there previously. Elwyn and I will attend the PM. We'll all meet later this morning and share our findings."

While the other team members returned to their desks, Elwyn followed Rachel back to her office.

"What time does Butterfield want us?" he asked.

"Not until ten, so there's time to grab a coffee first. What d'you think?" She posed in a short leather jacket. "It was Meggy's but she doesn't wear it anymore. Too young?" She twirled around to show it off.

"No. With those jeans, it looks good. You're looking a lot better these days," he said. "Less stressed, you know, after . . ."

"The debacle with McAteer?" She said for him and shrugged. "It's okay, Elwyn, I don't mind if you talk about it. Whether I like it or not, he's a fact of life, well, mine anyhow." She pulled a face.

He smiled a little sheepishly. "I don't like bringing it up, but it's been a couple of months now and you haven't mentioned him once."

"That's because it's an emotionally tricky subject." But she wasn't about to bore Elwyn with the details. "How's Marie?"

"Selling the house and happy to share the proceeds." He smiled. "Which means I can look at properties to buy. And it can't come soon enough, believe me. Life at my sister's has definitely lost its gloss."

Rachel and Elwyn had worked together for a long time and were close. Elwyn was the only member of Rachel's team who knew the truth about her and Jed McAteer. She never discussed personal issues with the others. Elwyn knew that she and McAteer had been an item in their teens and had seen each other periodically since. In the usual scheme of things this wouldn't have been a problem, but McAteer had once been a notorious villain. In recent times he'd become a property developer, enjoying a certain measure of success. He appeared to be trying hard to bury his past and reinvent himself, which was very laudable of course, but nevertheless Rachel did not want her name linked with his. Hence the secrecy. Elwyn also knew that McAteer was the biological father of Rachel's youngest daughter, Mia. As far as Rachel was concerned, that was one particular secret that must never come out.

The two of them made their way out of the building and down to the car park, where no one could overhear their conversation. "I think Alan's suspicious. Mia reckons he's being *off* with her." She threw Elwyn the keys to her car. "I don't know how, but I think he's found out that she's not his biological daughter. But whatever he thinks, Elwyn, I swear that if he takes it out on that girl, I'll have his guts!"

"No one knows, so how can he be?"

"You're forgetting something. Jed McAteer wants to be part of Mia's life. After all, he is her father. I wouldn't put it past him to make trouble just to spite me, and to suit his own ends."

CHAPTER THREE

Rachel averted her eyes from the body lying on the slab. She hated the morgue. Everything about it gave her the shivers. Being an only child, when her parents had died in a car crash it had been down to Rachel to identify the bodies. No matter how many times she came here, and it was often enough given her job, it never got any better.

"I'd say she's in her forties," Butterfield began. "There's some bruising to the face and upper body, not a vicious beating, more the result of fighting off her attacker." He took hold of the right hand. "There is bruising to her knuckles where she attempted to fight back. This here on her face is interesting." Butterfield indicated the place. "The bruising to the cheekbone suggests she was punched in the face, see? There's a cut just here."

"Any idea of what caused it?" Rachel asked.

"A ring on her attacker's finger would do it."

"If I found a suspect wearing a ring, could you match it?"

At that moment, Dr Judith Glover entered the room dressed in a white coverall. She was tall, of ample build and with short, no-nonsense grey hair. Jude didn't fuss over her appearance. She was a woman dedicated to her job, and her looks were unimportant as far as she was concerned.

Jude examined the wound. "We can certainly try for DNA. It's a deep cut. It bled, so traces will have been transferred to the ring. But don't leave it too long."

"Anything else, Jude?" asked Rachel.

"We didn't find the bullet in the trench, so I'm presuming it's still embedded in her brain. Once I have it, I should be able to tell you the type of gun they used."

Rachel nodded. "Beaten, and then shot through the head. So it's definitely murder."

"He wasn't kind, your killer," Butterfield said. "He's one sicko I wouldn't want to meet on a dark night." He continued with his external examination of the body. "There's no evidence of sexual assault."

"That's something at least. The clothes she was found in — will they help identify her?" Rachel asked.

"A simple navy skirt and shirt. If I had to guess, I'd say she was dressed for work. You can get clothes like that cheaply at any high street shop. I am curious about the lack of shoes though. We've found no sign of any so far," Jude said.

"Are we quite finished?" Butterfield said impatiently.

They watched as he examined her nose and throat.

"There is sand in the throat. She did not die immediately after being shot. However, she will only have lived for minutes, possibly seconds. The head wound was catastrophic."

They watched him take up a scalpel and make the customary incisions. "Non-smoker, evidence of minimal coronary artery disease." He removed the stomach. "Her last meal — nothing substantial, just the remains of an apple and chocolate."

"A busy woman with little time to eat properly," Elwyn said. "We miss meals all the time, and I often have a bar of chocolate in my pocket."

"Did your team find any of her belongings?" Rachel asked Jude. Butterfield's examination, though necessary, had told them very little about this woman.

Jude shook her head. "We've yet to examine her clothing, and my team are back at the site this morning, but nothing so far."

Butterfield looked up. "This might help you. She has a kidney missing. It's a neat job. She may have had a problem but the wound and her general state of health suggest she was a donor. Since she was a live donor, it's probable that a close relative was the recipient."

"When was this done?" asked Rachel.

"Within the last twelve months, I'd say."

It was a good place to start. They had a photo. If the transplant was done locally, it would have been at the Manchester Royal Infirmary.

"We'll do the usual tests, see if she was drugged or on medication," Jude said.

"An ordinary woman, no doubt living an ordinary life, and caring enough to give a loved one a kidney. Who did she cross to end up like this?" Rachel looked at Jude. "Anything and everything you can give me. I want to catch the bastard who did this."

"The second body will be more of a problem," Jude said. "We've determined very little so far. She's female, with long blonde hair and varnished finger and toenails. The decomposition will make establishing date of death difficult, but we'll do our best. Her clothes are interesting — a skirt and top made from a vivid red silky fabric. Perhaps she was on a night out when she met her untimely end."

"Any idea how long she'd been there?" Rachel asked.

"It's difficult to estimate, but I'd say two months, give or take," Jude said. "She wasn't buried particularly deep, the soil was simply piled on top of her body. The worms and other insects have had a field day, I'm afraid."

"Do you have any idea of her age?" Elwyn asked.

"The wisdom teeth hadn't erupted, so she was in her teens."

"PM on her?" Rachel asked.

"Tomorrow," Butterfield said. "I'm at a conference this afternoon."

"Meanwhile, I'll take samples and start my tests," added Jude.

"Do you know how she died?" asked Elwyn.

"Not for sure, but like our friend there," she nodded at the body on the table, "she has a suspicious hole in her skull, possibly from a bullet."

"Same method, then. I wonder if there's a link," Rachel said.

Jude shrugged. "Difficult to know. Once the PM and tests are done, you'll have a more complete picture."

To Rachel's relief, she and Elwyn were able to leave the mortuary.

"Two bodies, Elwyn," she said. "There has to be a link. They were found in the same spot, for goodness sake."

"You think it's someone's preferred dumping ground?"

"I don't know what to think. We'll take another look at the site later."

CHAPTER FOUR

By the time Rachel and Elwyn returned to the station, it was way past lunchtime. After pinning a photo of the murdered woman to the incident board, Rachel gathered the team for a briefing.

"Last night's victim tried to fight off her attacker. She has bruising to her hands and face, plus an impressive cut to her cheekbone, possibly from a ring. She was taken to that site and shot through the head. There is no doubt this was cold-blooded murder."

"Not a fight after a night out at the pub that ended badly, then," Jonny Farrell remarked.

"No, Jonny, the killer knew exactly what he was doing. But we do have something to go on. Our victim may have been a kidney donor. Jonny, contact the MRI and ask for the names of anyone who has had a transplant during the last year. There can't have been many with a live donor."

"And if they get all 'data protection' on me?"

"Then get a warrant first!" Rachel retorted. Really, sometimes the rules made no sense. "That'll take time, so impress on them that this is a murder enquiry, and as yet we haven't identified the victim."

"The building site, ma'am. It's owned by McAteer Developments." Jonny said.

Rachel saw the smirk and bristled. He couldn't know. How could he? Only Elwyn knew her secret, and she trusted him absolutely. Had there been rumours after the Brough case? Had Jonny re-read the case file and put two and two together? One smart comment and she'd have the DC for dinner!

"They're putting up a hundred affordable houses. I spoke to the project manager in their head office. The work has a tight budget and needs to run to time. Apparently there are penalties for each day handover is delayed."

"Are they aware of what's happened?" she asked indignantly.

"A member of the management team, a Liam Russell, is going down there this afternoon. He wasn't happy. Given that profit is pared to a minimum, he'd like this wrapping up swiftly."

She snorted. "My heart bleeds. These people, honestly, they've no idea. I want to know when this bloke turns up. I'll take a ride over and speak to him myself."

She turned to Amy, who was gazing intently at her mobile. "Any luck with the CCTV, DC Metcalfe?"

Amy glanced up with a surprised look on her face. "Sorry, ma'am. Just checking something."

Making arrangements for this evening more like. "Well? The CCTV?"

"The footage has been tampered with, ma'am. There's nothing from last night."

"What? Tampered with? Bollocks!" Rachel was furious. "Have you spoken to the site manager? I assume it's his responsibility?"

"He swears he has no idea how it happened. He went on about their system being hacked."

"Hacked, my . . ." Hands on her hips, Rachel shook her head. "It was deliberate, and I want action. Find out how that system works, and if periodic backups are taken. Who has access, you know the stuff. I want everyone who has visited that site during the last week interviewed — staff, delivery people, the lot."

"The site manager is keen to keep the killings quiet," Amy said. He's afraid that if word gets round, the houses won't sell."

Now Rachel was blazing. She looked down at the floor, tapping her toe. *Patience, girl* . . . She let the words run through her head. Finally, she faced the team. "Let's get one thing straight. I don't give a damn whether those houses sell or not. We have a job to do. See her?" She pointed at the photo of the victim. "Look at her face. Read the file, and see what was done to her. The trail is still hot, so we have a small window of opportunity. I need you giving this your complete attention and working at full tilt. We hit a blank wall, we find a way around it. Think, for God's sake! Use your initiative and let's catch this bastard!"

Rachel strode into her office, slamming the door behind her. She'd overreacted. It was the mention of that name. The second the word McAteer escaped Jonny's lips, she'd seen red. It wasn't the DC's fault, but still, Rachel had seen that smirk. What did Jonny know?

Elwyn opened the door. "Judith Glover has just rung in. She's down at the site and reckons we should join her."

"Okay, it's high on the 'to do' list anyway. You and me'll go."

"What's got into you?" he said. "That was over the top."

Rachel shook her head. "Sorry. It's him, Jed. He's back and causing trouble all over again. Will I never be free of that man?"

Elwyn closed the door behind him. "No, you won't, and you know perfectly well why. Whether you like it or not, he's part of your life now."

"Why does he have to be involved in every single case I touch these days? He haunts my life — at work and at home — like a bloody curse."

"Have you seen him since—?"

"No! And neither has Mia."

"Does she know the truth?"

Rachel stared at him. "No, she bloody doesn't. I haven't said anything, and he hasn't contacted her." She grabbed her jacket and pushed her mobile into one of the pockets. "I don't want her to know. I'm not ready for the harsh truth yet, and I doubt she is either."

"Jed McAteer is her father, Rachel. She has every right to know the truth."

"She's fourteen!" Rachel retaliated. "Telling her now would destroy her world. She loves Alan. As far as she's concerned, he's her dad. Apart from which, McAteer's a bloody crook. If he wasn't, we might have made a go of things years ago."

"He's not a crook now though, is he?" Elwyn said. "In fact, he's your archetypal Mister Respectable. Flourishing business, commands respect in his field. You could do worse."

Rachel took a breath. She could scarcely believe what she was hearing. "You're not suggesting that I get back together with him? For heaven's sake, Elwyn! He has a past. And, believe me, it'll raise its ugly head sooner or later. The man's a jailbird, he might even be a killer for all I know. And he knows some really dodgy people. I daren't risk my career over some teenage crush."

"He's more than that though, isn't he? You're still in love with him."

Of all the people Rachel knew, Elwyn was the only one who could get away with saying that. "Elwyn Price, if I had a handbag, I'd bloody well hit you with it!"

* * *

When they arrived at the site, Jude's team were hard at it, scraping and sifting the soil at the place where they'd found the two bodies.

"Don't step on that patch!" Jude shouted to them. "We think that's where the vehicle that brought last night's victim parked up. We've still to do casts of the tyre tracks and the footprints."

Fair enough. Rachel stared down at the hotchpotch of indentations on the muddy ground. How could anyone make sense of them?

"See this?" Jude pointed. "The van stops here and he pulls our victim from the back of the vehicle. He yanks her out by the arms, and her feet land here. The deeper indentations are where they hit the muddy ground."

Elwyn nodded. So far, so good.

"Then he drags her along to the trench."

Now she could picture it. Jude's description of events, complete with actions, made sense of the random marks on the ground.

"What about blood?" Rachel asked.

Jude smiled. "Now you have it. Last night I postulated that the victim was killed here. This makes me think I'm right. There is no blood along the tracks but plenty once we get to the trench." Jude moved a little nearer to where the body had been found. "She was shot about here and fell sideways into the trench." She pointed at the spot. "And that's where we find all the blood."

"Did she struggle?" Rachel asked.

"I'm checking that, but I suspect she was drugged and still only semi-conscious on arrival."

Elwyn nodded. "There's a car pulling up. This could be our person from McAteer's."

"Tell him to wait over there. We don't want him contaminating the scene," Rachel said.

"I'm planning to get some imaging equipment and see if there are any more surprises lurking in the ground," Jude said.

"Do that. Take as long as you need." Rachel looked around. Seen in daylight, it was a relatively small area. "How in hell's name do they expect to squeeze a hundred homes into this pocket handkerchief?"

"There won't be room to swing a cat, will there? But that's what they're all like nowadays. Profit rules, Rachel," Jude shook her head. "Look where we are, a spit away from central Manchester. They won't want to delay either. That site manager has been wittering on about the holdup all morning."

"Stuff their bloody profits. Finding our murderer comes first."

Rachel marched off to meet the man from McAteer's.

"Are you in charge?" she demanded.

He was tall, wore a business suit and clutched a new-looking briefcase. He gave Rachel a nervous smile and stuck out his hand.

"Liam Russell," he said.

He was softly spoken, and so obviously ill at ease that Rachel wondered how he got on with Jed. Jed McAteer usually went for go-getters. This one must have something going for him. Perhaps he was the acceptable face of the enterprise. After all, Jed had a reputation, and people have long memories.

"DCI Rachel King." She shook his hand. "There's still work to be done here. How much is anybody's guess. We have two bodies, and there may well be more. Until scenes-of-crime have finished their search, this site is off-limits, I'm afraid."

He paled visibly. "You mean people were killed here? My God."

"I'm afraid so. What was on this land before McAteer bought it?"

Liam Russell rummaged in his briefcase and retrieved a document. "Three shops and a small block of flats. The flats had been here since the sixties and were deemed unsafe."

"When was the site purchased?" she asked.

"Mr McAteer bought the site two years ago. The existing buildings were demolished, the land cleared and then it was left untouched until recently."

"How recently?"

"Building work started three weeks ago," he said.

So the older of the two bodies was left here before then.

CHAPTER FIVE

When Rachel and Elwyn returned to the station, they found Detective Chief Superintendent Harding standing in front of the incident board, staring at the photos of the two victims.

"I've had a call from Mr McAteer," he told Rachel. "He's concerned about the time it's taking to complete the search of his land. He's working to a tight schedule and is keen to make progress."

The warning bells sounded. She did not want McAteer having any contact with Harding. "He rang here? Spoke to you direct?" Rachel shook her head. "He's got some nerve, going behind my back. I'm the SIO on the case, he should direct all enquiries to me."

"I'm sure he didn't mean to circumnavigate protocol. The man's worried, that's all."

Rachel felt her temper rise again and took a deep breath to calm herself. It didn't work. "It's all about bloody profit with the likes of him! Well, he'll have to wait. One of the bodies we found has been there a while. For all we know, there could be more. We're far from finishing our search of that land," she paused, "sir."

Now she'd done it. She'd raised her voice, ranted at him. Given the mood he'd been in recently, he wasn't likely to react very well, was he?

"I take your point." Nodding, he turned and left the office. "Should he phone again, I'll direct him to you."

Rachel and Elwyn stood gazing after him, open-mouthed.

"What's up with him?" Elwyn asked. "He was actually reasonable for once. He didn't get on his high horse, he even sounded helpful. Is he on medication?"

Rachel laughed. "There are times when you crack me up, Elwyn. Let's hope he stays like that. McAteer could give us a problem."

"I think I've got somewhere with the donor aspect, ma'am," Jonny called from the next office. "Just over a year ago a woman donated a kidney to her sister. She fits the description, and the transplant was done at the MRI, like you thought."

"Do we have names?"

"The recipient was a Miss Anthea Moore. Her sister is one Agnes Moore. Anthea lives in Audenshaw."

"We'll go and see what she has to say. Have you tried to contact her?" Rachel asked.

"Yes, and she's at home all day. I didn't say anything about the body, as we're not yet sure if it is her sister."

"Good work," Rachel said. "The second body had been there a while. It will have been dumped after the site was cleared but before the builders moved in." She turned to Amy. "Anything on the CCTV?"

"The service provider will give us a backup copy. They're made hourly, so we still might get something."

"Good. When it comes through, get onto it straight away. And check any CCTV on the roads in that area. Concentrate on six thirty to eight last night. Come on, Elwyn. Off to Audenshaw."

* * *

Almost halfway between Manchester and Ashton, Audenshaw had good wide roads and a tramline that went right through to the city and the towns beyond.

"She lives along here somewhere," Elwyn said. "Take the next left."

The houses were pleasant semis with gardens, the only fly in the ointment being the noise from the busy A road they'd just driven in on.

Anthea Moore opened the front door and regarded them with a questioning stare. She seemed ill at ease. "What's this all about? Your young man didn't say much, just that you wanted to see me."

She was about fifty, tall, straight-backed with greying hair. She wasn't smiling.

"I'm DCI King and this is DS Pryce. We're from East Manchester CID." Rachel paused for a moment, seeking out similarities between this woman and their victim. As far as she could see, they looked nothing like each other. Their victim had been an attractive woman, Anthea looked hard. "We're here to ask you some questions about your sister, Agnes."

The woman eyed the pair with suspicion. "What questions? What do you think Agnes has done?"

"Possibly nothing, but we'd like a word anyway."

"You're wasting your time. Agnes isn't here, she's on holiday."

Her voice faltered — nerves, Rachel decided, as she watched the woman rub at the sleeves of her sweater.

"Perhaps you could help us to get one or two things straight."

Anthea Moore nodded. "If I can."

"I believe you received a kidney from Agnes about a year ago."

"Yes, and I was truly grateful, it was wonderful of Agnes, doing that for me. There's just the two of us you see, so we're especially close."

"Did she live here with you?" Elwyn asked her.

Anthea didn't seem to pick up on his use of the past tense. "No, Agnes has a flat in town, that development in New Islington. It's more convenient for her work."

"Have you seen Agnes recently?" Rachel asked.

"No, I told you, she's on holiday, a tour of the Algarve. She left on Tuesday, and she'll be gone another week." Anthea shifted from foot to foot and rubbed at her side. "What's this about? All these questions about Agnes, what's happened?"

"When did you last speak to her?"

"Monday night. She dropped her cat off — I'm looking after it for her."

"Do you have a photo of Agnes?"

"Why?" She looked from one detective to the other. "Agnes is fine, she's not in any trouble."

"We hope so, Anthea, but it would help to see a photo."

"You'd better come in."

They followed Anthea inside.

She picked up a framed photo from the coffee table. "This is us a few months ago, at a friend's wedding."

This was the part of the job that Rachel disliked the most, having to deliver bad news. She was already picturing this woman's horror when she heard the news. Staring back at Rachel, and smiling happily, was their victim. There was no use wrapping it in cotton wool. Straight out with it was always the best way.

"I'm sorry, Anthea, but your sister was found dead this morning. We believe she was murdered." Rachel gave her a moment or two to take this in. "I'm really sorry for your loss. I'm going to need your help to catch her killer."

There was a look of utter disbelief on Anthea Moore's face. She stared back at Rachel, her eyes blazing. "Agnes? Dead? I don't believe it! She can't be, not my sister. I don't know why you've come here with this pack of lies, trying to frighten me." She picked up a mobile phone that was lying on the coffee table. "I'll ring her now. You'll see — Agnes is out in the sun, enjoying herself. Anyway, who would want to kill her? You're off your heads. You people have no idea what you're doing, do you?"

Rachel and Elwyn stood back and waited. Anthea had the phone clamped to her ear, her eyes growing wider with each passing second.

After what seemed an age, she shouted, "No!" and threw the phone to the floor. "Why Agnes? It doesn't make any sense. She's never harmed anyone."

"She was killed here in Manchester, on a patch of land in Beswick."

"She works — worked — in Beswick." Anthea dabbed at the tears running down her cheeks. "Agnes was a nurse at a GP practice, the health centre on Ashton Old Road. Been there years, she had. Knew everyone in the area."

"You saw her on Monday night." Elwyn was busy writing all this down. "When was she due to fly out?"

"Tuesday morning. Early, she said."

"We'll need her address," Rachel said gently. "And a key if you have one. How old was Agnes?"

"Forty-five."

"Was she married or in a steady relationship?" Rachel asked.

"No. Neither of us ever met the right man." Anthea looked away and began fiddling with her sleeves again. "Mind you, Agnes could be secretive. There may have been someone she didn't tell me about."

Rachel wondered why her question had made Anthea so nervous. "We'll have to speak to you again. Do you work, Anthea?"

"I teach at the academy in Ancoats. School hours that's where you'll find me."

"Thank you, that's very helpful."

"Can I see her?" Anthea asked in a small voice.

"Yes, of course. One of my officers will accompany you. I'll send a car round to pick you up this afternoon. Do you have anyone who can be with you?"

"The woman next door will come in. She'll sort me out."

Rachel and Elwyn left Anthea standing in the middle of the room, absent-mindedly rubbing the back of her neck.

"What d'you think?" Elwyn asked, once they were outside.

"She's hiding something, but I'm not sure what. She was certainly nervous. We'll let her get over the shock and then talk to her again."

CHAPTER SIX

"Our victim is Agnes Moore. She was forty-five, and a nurse at a GP practice in Beswick." Rachel looked up from her notes to see that Harding had come in and was standing at the back. He never did this, so why all the interest now? He looked thinner than usual and pale. Was he worried about something, the case perhaps? It crossed her mind that Jed might have offered him a backhander to speed things up, but dismissed the notion. All her instincts told her that Harding was straight.

"Her sister will identify the body later today," she continued. "I'll visit Agnes's work place and speak to her colleagues. Meanwhile, I want forensics at her flat in New Islington and a complete background check." She looked at Jonny. "Did we get the plans for that site from the council?"

"Yes, they emailed them. I'm no expert, but it looks like the bloke from McAteer's was correct — flats and shops, all long past their sell-by date. Are we proceeding on the assumption that the killings are linked, ma'am?"

Harding was still standing there. His presence was making her twitchy. "Can I help you, sir?"

"Yes. You can meet with me and Mr McAteer later today. My office at six." Having dropped that little bombshell, he left.

Rachel had to remind herself that Harding didn't *know*. He was simply reacting to an annoyed punter who was losing money because of their investigation. But that didn't help the nerves. What the hell was Jed up to? Plus, there was no precedent for this. Rachel could not recall any instance in the past when a senior officer had invited the owner of a crime scene in to reassure them.

Rachel shook herself. Back to the investigation. "Both bodies were found within a spit of each other, so they're quite possibly connected. But until we know a great deal more about Agnes and her life, we can't be sure." She looked at Amy. "Agnes and Anthea Moore are your project, Amy. Agnes was a nurse at the health centre, Anthea's a teacher at Ancoats Academy. Find out everything you can about them. Anthea told us that neither of them was in a relationship but dig into that, and make it thorough. I suspect Anthea's hiding something. I want to know who their friends were, where they spent their free time — the lot. Agnes appears to have been whiter than white, but she upset someone badly enough for them to kill her. There were no belongings at the scene. Check her bank account and find out if it's been used since she was murdered."

Rachel glanced at her watch. It was after four p.m. and she'd had nothing to eat. "Elwyn. Canteen. A quick bite and then we'll visit Agnes's workplace."

They took the stairs to the canteen. "It's good to see your appetite back after all the events of the last few months," Elwyn said on their way up.

"I'm fine. I just wish that Jed would butt out of my life. What's he up to, Elwyn? I feel like the man's stalking me."

"It could be a genuine beef. He does stand to lose money if he doesn't meet his deadline."

"I know him," Rachel said. "That development isn't the sort of thing Jed usually bothers with. I'll lay odds he took it on knowing the deadlines were so tight. It'll be a tax dodge. He loses money and offsets the amount against the huge profits he rakes in elsewhere. The apartments in that

31

block he built in Castlefields are changing hands for a million plus. I know he hung onto two of those as an investment. He doesn't go for the cheaper end of the market, Elwyn, so there must be something up."

They sat at the back of the canteen, against the wall, watching the comings and goings. Jonny Farrell had followed in their wake and was at the counter ordering food.

"What is it with him?" Rachel asked. "Have you noticed the clothes? He dresses like he's got money to burn."

Elwyn smiled. "What? You mean you don't know?"

"Know what?" Rachel had her eyes on the menu.

"His dad's Bobby Farrell, the footballer."

Rachel shrugged. "Soz, Elwyn, you know I don't do football."

He laughed. "This city has two of the biggest teams in the country, and you don't do football!"

"Do you?" Rachel asked. "I've never heard you going on about matches, goals and so on like the others do."

"You've got me there. Guess I'm always too busy."

"Go on. This dad of his — good, is he?"

"He played for both City and United in his time. He must have made a fortune. And that's why our bright young thing is so spectacularly dressed. It'll be Daddy's money he's spending."

"With that behind him, I wonder why Jonny wanted to join the force in the first place," she mused.

"Why did any of us?"

She smiled. "As for you, it's in your DNA. Your dad was CID. In my case, I always wanted to chase criminals. Ever since my teens, I could never see myself doing anything else."

"What you having?" Elwyn took the menu from her.

"A sandwich and coffee will do for now, then we'll get off to that health centre in Beswick."

* * *

The health centre wasn't what Rachel had expected. In her own village of Poynton, the local practice would be full of mums and tots at this time of day. This one was full of individuals who looked as if they needed a damn good meal and a wash. A number of men and a couple of teenage girls were waiting their turn, staring at nothing. In the corner, a man was slumped over a newspaper, snoring.

Rachel approached the receptionist and produced her warrant card. "Do you have a practice manager we could speak to?"

"Yes, Lorraine Hughes. I'll get her."

"What d'you reckon's going on here, Elwyn?"

"If I had to make a guess, I'd say rough sleepers come here to get some shelter and warmth."

"I wonder whose idea that was?"

The receptionist beckoned to them. "Lorraine's office is just down here."

"Well, this is very mysterious," Lorraine Hughes said. "Is there something wrong?"

"I'm DCI King and this is DS Pryce. We're here about Agnes Moore." Rachel produced a photo from her pocket. "I understand she worked here?"

"Yes, but you won't be able to talk to her. She's on holiday."

"I'm afraid that's not the case," Elwyn said.

"I don't understand, did she miss her plane or something?"

"I'm very sorry but Agnes has been murdered," Elwyn said.

Lorraine looked away. Her eyes seemed to be searching the room for something to fix on, anything but the two detectives. Rachel wondered why. Was she hiding something?

After a lengthy silence, Lorraine said, "Are you sure it's our Agnes?"

"Yes, we are," Rachel said. "When was the last time you saw her?"

"Monday teatime, as usual. We were both on the early shift. After work she came to my house to borrow a suitcase. I only live up the road. We had a chat and a coffee. She left about five, as I recall." Lorraine Hughes frowned. "You surely can't think I had anything to do with her murder?"

"No. We're simply trying to build up a picture of her last movements," Rachel said. "Was Agnes popular?"

Lorraine looked away again, frowning, apparently considering how to answer the question.

"Not always. She could be harsh at times."

"What do you mean?" Rachel asked. 'Harsh?' What didn't she want to say?

Lorraine continued to avoid her gaze.

"Mostly people liked Agnes because she was helpful. She got on with the job. I can't think of anyone who'd want to harm her," she said.

"Well, someone did," Rachel said bluntly. "But it still doesn't answer the question."

"People didn't always appreciate Agnes's help," Lorraine said. "Sometimes it got her into trouble — and I was held responsible. Some of the other staff thought her methods a little odd."

"What d'you mean?" Rachel asked.

"You saw that lot in the waiting room today. That's down to Agnes. She visited the homeless hostel up the road and a couple of other places, did health checks and the like. Unfortunately, it backfired somewhat. We don't treat people unless they are registered here as patients. We don't turn people away, you can always register as a temporary patient, and we'll even give this address as your temporary home. But we have to follow the rules, our funding depends on it. Agnes didn't always go by the regulations, and it often got her into trouble. Apart from which, all the homeless people who are feeling the cold come and sit in the waiting room. It puts the other patients off."

"Can you think of anyone in particular that got annoyed by it?" Rachel asked.

"No, not really, it's just a bit inconvenient," Lorraine said. "At busy times seats are in short supply, and they can get a bit rowdy. A lot of them out there are on drugs. Their hygiene leaves a lot to be desired. They get drunk and angry, and they annoy people by asking for money."

"There are a couple of young girls waiting. What's their story?" Elwyn asked.

"Much the same. They'll be rough sleepers too. The young girls trusted Agnes. They were her special project. She offered contraception advice and the like."

"How did Agnes deal with the troublemakers?" Rachel asked.

Lorraine seemed to freeze. "There's been no one in particular bothering Agnes, if that's what you're getting at. We have cameras, and we've contracted a security firm. Any trouble, it just takes a phone call or someone to press the alarm button and we can have them removed."

"In that case why not get them to clear the waiting room?" Rachel asked.

"We don't like turning people away."

"How do the other staff feel about treating them?" Elwyn asked.

"If someone's registered, they don't have much choice. If anyone at the hostel has a problem, they send them here. Another initiative of Agnes's." Lorraine grimaced. "One of the doctors runs a clinic three times a week. He tries to help. Well, we all do what we can. But Agnes was the driving force behind all our efforts."

"She sounds like a good woman, the sort who should have been popular," Rachel remarked. "Do you know who her friends were? If she went out much?"

Lorraine shrugged. "I've no idea. We chatted and went for the occasional drink and, like I said, she borrowed my suitcase. But that was it."

"Was she close to anyone else here?" Rachel said.

"I don't think so, apart from that sister of hers. Kept herself private, did Agnes. Look, I really can't help you, and I need to get on."

Rachel stood up. "Thanks for your help."

As soon as they were outside, Rachel said, "We'll visit that hostel up the road."

"Not now we won't," Elwyn said. "Have you seen the time? It'll take us thirty minutes at least to get back to the station. Look at that road, it's chocka."

Rachel thought of the meeting looming ahead and groaned. "You're right. I'd better not keep Harding waiting. They're not going to like what I have to tell them as it is. We're not leaving that site until Jude is absolutely sure there are no more bodies there."

They were just getting into the car when she saw a teenage girl waving at them. Rachel was certain she hadn't seen her in the waiting room.

"Is Agnes okay?" the girl called out.

"Do you know her?" Rachel asked.

"Yes. She promised to help me. I've been looking for her."

The girl was skimpily dressed, in a short red skirt and matching crop top. She walked towards them, shivering, her arms around her flat chest. But the most striking thing about the girl was her bright pink hair hanging in strands around her face. Her eyes were dark, hollow. Rachel wondered if she was on something.

"Do you go to the hostel?" she asked.

The girl shook her head. "Look, I shouldn't have spoken to you. I have to go." Abruptly, she turned and legged it up the road.

Elwyn watched her go. "Interesting. I got the impression that young lady had a lot more to say."

"She was scared. Did you see her eyes? She didn't take them off the passing traffic. She was worried stiff in case she was seen talking to us. We need to go after her, Elwyn, get her to speak to us. Find out how she knew Agnes. She might be able to help us."

"You haven't got time now, Rachel. That meeting with Harding won't wait. We'll come back," Elwyn said. "Then we'll go through the houses and businesses up and down this street like a dose of salts. Someone will know her."

CHAPTER SEVEN

Ruby was tired. She felt as if she'd been running for miles. In order to avoid the police, she'd dodged in and out of the side streets and alleyways. Confident she'd lost them, she leaned against a shop wall, gasping for breath. They were looking for Agnes. Something must've happened to her. The policewoman hadn't said anything specific, but Ruby knew it couldn't be good — otherwise why would they be here? She felt sick. This was all her fault. If only she hadn't asked Agnes for help.

A car drew to a halt at the kerbside. "What the hell d'you think you're doing, running round like that?" the driver shouted. "Get in the bloody car!"

Shaking with fear, Ruby clambered into the passenger seat. "My medication isn't ready yet," she lied. "The woman in the health centre said to hang on, but I was suffocating in that waiting room."

"Lying little cow! You were talking to that bitch from the police."

"I didn't say anything! I wouldn't." A sharp blow to the side of her head made her cry out in pain.

"You'd better not be lying to me. We have an arrangement, and despite what you think has happened, that still stands."

"I needed to see the nurse, that's all," she whined. "Please don't hurt me."

"Why? What the hell's wrong with you? You know the drill. You're unwell, you come to me first."

"My shoulder, Nicu . . . you know how it gets."

"I'll give you something when we get back," he said.

Ruby closed her eyes. She could see no way out of this nightmare. The last time she'd spoken to Agnes, she had offered her a safe place to stay and help to get free. Only now did Ruby realise what an opportunity this had been. But she'd let it slip through her fingers. Agnes had warned her about the people she worked for. They were brutal, she said. And they were.

"Carry on like this, dodging off every chance you get, and you know what'll happen," he was saying.

"Oh? What's that? The same as happened to some of the others?" Ruby shrank back into the seat, dreading his reaction. "Take that blonde girl. One day she was fine, the next she was gone. I can't get my head round it. How can I if you don't tell me anything?"

But the expected blow didn't come. "You all know the score, don't break the rules. Take it as a warning. Keep your head down, do as you're told and we'll all be happy. It's dead simple. An idiot could do it."

Ruby's mind was in turmoil. The rumours about what had happened to the blonde girl were flying around. One of the other girls said she'd been killed. The thought of it made Ruby sick with fear. And now Agnes was missing and couldn't help her either. One thing was certain, one way or another, she had to get free.

* * *

Rachel ran her long fingers through her unruly red hair and stared at her reflection in the mirror. She needed some make-up — something to give her face a bit of colour, lift the pallor. Trouble was, she didn't usually wear any, so had none with her. She could ask Amy Metcalfe, she supposed, but decided against it. It would only cause gossip in the office. Rooting through her desk drawer, she found an old lipstick of Megan's. She'd no idea how it got there, but it would have to do. She slicked a coat of the deep pink shade across her mouth and took another look in the mirror. Not bad. Not as glamourous as Jed McAteer was probably used to these days, but did she really care? She sighed. The answer was yes, as always. Part of her still loved him. Rachel closed her eyes. *Silly bitch. The man takes care of number one, you know that. He doesn't give a damn about you or what you look like.*

"You look knockout," Elwyn said when she passed through the main office. "Don't take any flack. Stick to your guns."

"I will, don't you worry. That site is ours until I say different. And as for the flattery, all that'll get you is a kick up the backside, DS Pryce." She giggled at him.

Minutes later, she was nervously tapping on Harding's door. She'd not seen Jed since Mia's kidnapping. Well, she had to hand it to him, he did deserve credit for being on the ball that day. It was down to him that Mia had been saved. The bottom line was, she owed him. Nevertheless, he was an irritant she didn't need. The job was hard enough without the added complication of an ex-lover who also happened to be a criminal.

"DCI King," Harding said. "Do take a seat."

The two men were seated at a small round table by the window. Since it was the only free chair, she had no choice but to sit next to Jed.

"You've met Mr McAteer before, I believe," Harding began.

Rachel's heart missed a beat. *What did Harding know?*

"During the Brough case," he continued.

Oh, relief. He must have read it in a report.

A half smile on his lips and a twinkle in his eyes, Jed McAteer sipped at his coffee as if he didn't have a care in the world. He looked Rachel up and down before giving her a nod.

"When can I have my site back?" he said. "I don't want to cause hassle, but every day lost leaves a real dent in my budget."

Rachel immediately saw red. "Don't you mean *profit*, Mr McAteer?"

"We've been contracted to do a job. We work to time. If the final product is up to scratch, the families who eventually live in those houses get a good deal. We have people waiting to move in. We meet with delays and the cost will inevitably rise, and then everybody loses."

"Two bodies were found on that land," she said, trying to avoid his gaze. "One had been there for some time. Our forensic people need to make sure that there are no others and gather all the evidence available. That will take a day or two, I'm afraid, and there's nothing we can do about it."

She saw the look. Jed was trying to keep that temper of his under control. If they hadn't been in Harding's office, he'd have let rip.

He was silent for a few moments. Then he tried a different tack. "Perhaps I can help. We have plenty of heavy lifting and digging gear. Anything you need, just give me a call."

He accompanied the offer with a charming smile that made her stomach lurch. Damn him! Rachel leaned back in her chair. Why did he have to come across as so bloody reasonable and look so good doing it? She had no doubt in her mind that this offer was for Harding's benefit. "That's good of you," she said. "I will speak to forensics in the morning and let you know what they say."

"Is there any possibility that we can work on part of the site?" he asked.

Rachel sighed. "Until we know for sure that there are no more bodies, the answer has to be no. We are as keen as you are to get this wrapped up, Mr McAteer, but the search will have to run its course, I'm afraid."

"Well, all I can say is that a swift conclusion to this would be appreciated."

"Is that all, sir?" Rachel asked Harding. He nodded.

Rachel couldn't wait to get out of there. With a hasty, "Have a good evening, gentlemen," she closed the door behind her.

* * *

The main office was empty except for Elwyn, who was still at his desk. "What is McAteer doing cosying up to Harding? I don't know what's going on in that twisted mind of his, but I don't like it one bit."

"Money, Rachel. I've been checking up on McAteer and he's made a substantial donation to the police benevolent fund."

"Slimy little git! So that's his plan, is it? Buy his reputation back. He won't get far with that. The man's a villain and villains don't change."

"What have you agreed to?" Elwyn asked.

"Nothing much. He's offered the use of the equipment on the site, should we need it." She flopped down beside Elwyn. "I'm sick of this. He worms his way in, buys Harding's respect with a load of cash and we've suddenly got to toe the line. What is it with him? What's his secret? No one sees through him. Everyone he meets these days thinks he's Mister Wonderful!"

"You're tired. It's been a long day. You should go home and have a rest. Tomorrow we've got the PM on the other body and the search for the girl with pink hair."

"Don't you stay too late either." She stood up and looked over his shoulder. "What've you got there?"

"It's the brochure for those houses McAteer's building. The specs look good and they're in a convenient position for work."

Rachel stared at him, aghast. "You have to be joking! You'd buy a house from Jed McAteer?"

"They're in my price range, Rachel. I can't afford to be choosy."

"Just make sure you know what you're doing. I wouldn't trust him if I were you. The man's a weasel!"

* * *

It was a good half hour's drive to Rachel's home in the Cheshire village of Poynton. When she and Alan had divorced, she'd bought a couple of rundown semi-detached cottages, planning to knock them into one and do them up. But it hadn't happened. Work, stress and money dictated that the first cottage was sorted but the second was put on the market, and to her surprise, Alan had bought it. That was several years ago now, and Rachel had got over her initial irritation at having her ex right next door. As it turned out, it was damn useful.

Tonight, he'd made dinner and was sitting with Mia at her kitchen table, both of them poring over her homework.

"Quadratic equations," he said. "As I recall, there's some sort of formula to solve them."

"Don't ask me. All that weird maths stuff evaporated out of my brain years ago." She looked at Mia. "Go and google it."

Mia gathered up her books and went out.

"I was waiting for you," Alan said, once they were alone. "I thought we could have that talk."

Rachel groaned inwardly. She had no energy left for a fight with Alan. If he did know about McAteer, he'd end up ranting, and she was not in the mood.

"Does it have to be now?" she said.

"It's important."

She sat down opposite him. "Okay, but if you're going to get angry, shelve it. I don't want Mia upsetting."

"There's nothing to get angry about," he said. "It's just a bit tricky, that's all."

Oh, so it wasn't what she'd thought. Rachel was intrigued.

He coughed, sounding embarrassed. "I've met someone. I've been seeing her for a while, actually. She's nice, you'll like her."

42

Rachel certainly hadn't expected that. She smiled at him and poured herself a glass of wine from the bottle on the table. "That's a relief. We were beginning to wonder what we'd done. Mia thinks you've been off with her — she was having a go at breakfast. But it's to do with your new lady friend, isn't it? You're afraid the kids might not approve."

"I'm terrified, to be honest. Belinda was coming round this evening but I put her off. I wanted to tell you first."

"You don't have to explain yourself to me, Alan. I think it's great news," Rachel said. "Do you want me to tell the girls?"

"It might be better coming from you. I thought the three of you could come to mine for tea tomorrow and meet Belinda."

"That would be good. Don't worry, I'm sure the girls will be fine about it."

"Good. Well, I'll get off now, if you're okay." He bent down and kissed her cheek.

Rachel was gobsmacked. Up until recently, she'd firmly believed that Alan wanted her back. Seems she was way off beam. What a relief. Despite having been divorced for a few years now, she'd never really felt like a free woman.

CHAPTER EIGHT

Day Two

"There's a homeless hostel on Ashton Old Road, Beswick,"
Rachel told her team. "I want it checking out. Jonny,
Amy, make that your task for the morning. Take note of
the clientele and speak to the staff. Agnes tried to help the
people who use it. She arranged for them to attend the health
centre if they had a problem. Find out if she was involved
with anyone in particular — if she was liked, if the regulars
trusted her. Also check if many women or young girls use
the shelter." She was thinking of the girl who'd approached
them yesterday.

"Rachel?" Elwyn tapped his computer screen. "Agnes's
debit card has been used. This morning, at an ATM in
Beswick."

"Get onto the bank, see if they have cameras. Find out
Agnes's financial details while you're at it."

"Don't forget the PM," he said.

Rachel checked her watch. "I'll get down there now.
Join me when you can."

Rachel had a lot on her mind, not least the fact that
whoever had used that card must know Agnes's PIN. Did

that mean she'd been forced to reveal it? Perhaps they had her bag and had found it written down somewhere.

They had two bodies. Her gut told her there had to be a connection, but how? With luck, the PM would reveal sufficient details about the other body to give them a start. It was a big ask, but Jude was a brilliant forensic specialist. Rachel hurried out towards her car.

* * *

"You know what, Rachel? The old saying that the dead cannot speak is utterly wrong," Jude said. "The forensic evidence is there, we just have to find it. We already know she was young, blonde and took care of her appearance." Rachel gave her a questioning look. Jude smiled. "The nail varnish."

She certainly wasn't pleasant to look at now. Two months in the soil had wreaked havoc. Some of the decomposing soft tissue was already separating from the bones, and the smell was something else.

"It's difficult to tell from the state she's in, but I think she was a pretty little thing," Butterfield remarked. "She has good facial bone structure. There is no doubt in my mind that she died from a bullet wound in the head. I will look carefully at what's left of the brain and see if I can find a bullet." He pointed to a hole in the back of her skull. "It went in here," he said. "And there is another hole here, in the temple."

"Exit wound?" Rachel asked.

"Possibly." He looked at Jude. "If the bullet isn't in the body, do a further search of that trench. It's possible she was knocked to the ground, shot at close range and the bullet passed straight through.

"We are combing every inch of that area," Jude said. "If there is a bullet, we'll find it. There's no sign of a gun, so I guess the killer took it away with him."

"I'd like to know if both this girl and Agnes were killed with the same gun," Rachel said. "Both shot and left within inches of each other — it's just too much of a coincidence."

"Best not jump to conclusions yet," Jude said.

"Did you find anything else?" Rachel mentally crossed her fingers. She needed something to go on.

"The remnants of her clothing are interesting," Jude said. "A short skirt and crop top made from a scarlet silky fabric. It looked like a type of uniform, but where from is anyone's guess."

Rachel immediately thought of the girl with pink hair who'd spoken to them outside the health centre. She was wearing clothes matching this description. Did she work at the same place?

"Can we be sure she's been dead two months?" Rachel asked Butterfield.

He shrugged. "Not really."

"But we've found something else that might help," Jude added. "We found this under the body. She may have been holding it when she was killed."

Jude held up an evidence bag containing a dirty scrap of paper.

"It's very wet and the print has faded, but you can just make out the address at the top. It came from the Medical Centre in Beswick. It looks like an appointment card to me. It's difficult to read, but it's dated this year. We've photographed it and enhanced it as best we can. I'll put it in the report, of course, but in the meantime, I'll text you a copy."

It was a start.

"There's another thing too," Jude said. "When I was examining Agnes Moore's clothes I found this in the pocket of her skirt."

Jude held up a second evidence bag. This one contained a necklace, a fine gold chain with a flat gold heart hanging from it.

"There's an inscription," Jude said. "It simply reads, 'Agnes' with an 'X' underneath it. A kiss?"

Rachel's mind was racing. "She hid it. Took it off and put it in her pocket, out of sight. It must've been important to her."

Jude smiled. "Possibly. It's new, the hallmark on the heart confirms that."

"A present from someone?" Rachel said.

"A heart," Jude added. "That probably means a man."

Jude was probably right. Rachel took a couple of photos of it with her mobile. "I'll see if her workmates know anything about it. I doubt whether her sister will."

"Agnes's clothing had a lot of small fibreglass strands caught in it," Jude said.

"Where would they have come from?" Rachel asked.

"You know the type that comes in a roll? It's used for roofing insulation. They were possibly picked up from the vehicle that transported her to the site."

"Thanks, Jude, that is useful." Rachel smiled at her. Jude had given them quite a few leads.

"We'll be able to get DNA from the girl, if you find someone you want me to try and match." Jude nodded at the slab. "I'm still running tests on this one. It's sad, isn't it? I wonder if anyone is missing her."

Butterfield had been quietly getting on with the post-mortem. "She's given birth," he suddenly announced examining the pelvis.

An added complication. "I wonder what happened to the infant?" Rachel said. "Can you tell if she went to full term?"

Butterfield shrugged. "Difficult to say."

"If she did give birth, she may have had help to arrange foster care or adoption, or a relative may have the child. Perhaps that's what the appointment was for." Jude nodded at the scrap of paper in the evidence bag. "I'll get as good an image as I can for you."

Rachel glanced at her watch. She'd check with the health centre, see if they had any record.

"She has two healed rib fractures," Butterfield said, "inflicted no more than two years ago."

Rachel sighed. This girl, whoever she was, had lived a hard life. So what chance would her offspring have? "A beating?"

"You know I can't tell that," Butterfield said. "It is a possibility, but they could just as easily have been caused by a fall. She's had a broken arm too. There is a fracture of the radius that is several years old."

Rachel had heard enough. The girl was too young to have lived such a hard and painful life. Her history was crucial to finding out why she died.

"Thanks, Jude. I'll leave you to it."

This case just got more complicated. Agnes and the girl had both been killed in the same way, so Agnes's murder wasn't random. It looked like they had a serial killer on their hands.

* * *

Back in her car, Rachel rang Elwyn. "I'm still at the morgue, and I've had a break of sorts. Agnes had a necklace hidden in a pocket of her skirt. I'm off to see her sister and then the health centre, see if anyone recognises it. An appointment card from there was found underneath the older body. I'll ask about that too."

"Is the necklace important?" he asked.

"It's actually a chain with a heart-shaped pendant. It has her name on it, with a kiss. It may have been given to her by a man. That's worth investigating. From what Jude has turned up, I reckon the same killer murdered both women. Both were shot in the head."

"That's not good, Rachel. I hope they don't find any more bodies."

"Where are you?" she asked.

"I'm still at the bank," he said. "They're dragging their heels about granting access to the footage. I'll ring you when I get it."

Rachel made her way to Audenshaw. She hadn't rung ahead and just hoped that Anthea would be in. She was getting out of the car when a neighbour called out to her.

"I heard what happened. Dreadful business. It's really upset that one." She nodded at Anthea's door. "She's taken it badly. It's made her a nervous wreck."

"Not surprising," Rachel said. "It was her sister."

"Don't be fooled. They didn't always get on — argued like mad at times. Strong personalities, the pair of them, particularly Anthea. She didn't approve of Agnes's job, or her friends come to that."

That sparked Rachel's interest. "Which friends in particular, do you know?"

But the neighbour didn't have time to reply. Anthea appeared at the front door. "Do you want me?"

"I'd like another word," Rachel said.

"I've told you everything I can," Anthea said. "It's upsetting, all this interrogation."

"I'm not interrogating you, Anthea. I simply want to find who killed your sister." Rachel followed Anthea inside, took her mobile from her pocket and showed her the photos of the necklace. "Do you recognise this?"

Anthea backed away, staring at Rachel. "Was it him? Did he do it?"

"Who, Anthea?"

"I kept telling her he was no good. He's been inside, you know, and he's a druggie. But Agnes wouldn't listen. She said I was jealous, that he was a different man now."

"Why didn't you tell me about him before?" Rachel asked.

Anthea looked away. "I don't know. I suppose I was afraid. He's dangerous. I've only met him once and we didn't get on. I needed time to think."

"His name, Anthea." Rachel was losing patience with the woman. "I need a name."

"Don Akerman."

"Where will I find him?" Rachel asked.

"At the homeless hostel. He works there."

Rachel went back to her car and rang the incident room. She spoke to Stella, the information officer. "Look up a Don

Akerman on the system. He's done time. I want to know what for and when. Text the info to me."

She rang Jonny. "There's a man called Akerman working at the hostel. He was close to Agnes. Don't let him know you're interested, just keep an eye on him. I'm on my way."

CHAPTER NINE

"I hate this part of town," Amy said. "It's old and dirty, and needs all the rejuvenation it can get. If you ask me, those houses McAteer's building will enhance round here no end."

"It does look a bit rough," Jonny shouted, struggling to make himself heard above the roar of the traffic. "Noisy too. That was the boss, she's going to join us. There's a bloke works here we're to keep an eye on."

"Doesn't trust us to question him ourselves, I suppose," Amy complained. "What is it with her? I want to go for sergeant, but that'll never happen with that one on my case."

But Jonny wasn't listening. His attention had been drawn to two men arguing outside the rundown building that housed the hostel. One looked ready to punch the other. Jonny jumped out and ran over to them.

"Whoa, mate, take a step back." Jonny pulled the smaller of the two away. He had what looked like blood all down the front of his T-shirt, but on closer inspection, Jonny realised it was soup. "I'd go back in and get cleaned up if I was you," he said.

"He's barred!" bellowed a woman from the hostel doorway. "He's a troublemaker, and we can do without the aggro."

51

The woman's hefty build matched with her voice. She wore a smudged white overall and had a tea towel draped over one shoulder. Her podgy face was made no slimmer by a mass of dry bleached hair. "We're busy serving the poor buggers a hot dinner when he comes in and starts throwing his weight about." She stared at Jonny for a moment. "You're police, aren't yer? Tell you lot a mile off. Sort him, will yer, then come in and I'll give you a cuppa."

Amy giggled. "Too good an invitation to pass up."

"Is there somewhere else you can go to clean up?" Jonny asked the man.

"Mate down the road," he muttered, and staggered off.

Jonny and Amy went inside. The place was full. A dozen tables filled the small room and there must have been fifty or more people seated around them, all eating hungrily.

"Over here!" the woman called out. "Mavis Smithson, Supervisor." She plonked two mugs of tea on the counter. "Fill your boots. There's sugar over there."

"We're looking for a Mr Akerman. Does he work here?" Amy asked.

"Don? Yes, he's the manager, but it's his day off today." She eyed the two of them suspiciously. "Why, what d'you think he's done?"

"We'd like a word, that's all." Jonny smiled at her.

"Don't soft soap me, laddie. I know about Don's past. He's been inside. He's got a reputation." She leaned towards Jonny. "But you've got to be hard to survive in this place. Otherwise the punters will walk all over you."

"A word won't hurt, surely?" Amy said.

Rachel had made it to the hostel in record time. "Right. Where is he?" She strode up to the counter and showed Mavis Smithson her warrant card. "I'd help us if I were you."

Mavis smirked at Jonny. "She the boss? Well, God help you!"

"Don't make me get heavy," Rachel retorted.

"Well he's not here," Mavis said. "And I'm not bloody psychic."

"His address then. We need a word urgently."

"Hassle, hassle. Gets more than his fair share, does Don. He doesn't do anything to deserve it either. Sure, he's been inside but he's a changed man now. He's not like he was." Reluctantly, Mavis handed Rachel a card with Akerman's address on it.

* * *

"Amy, get back to the station and check Akerman's background. I want to know what he was in for, who he was involved with, and what he's been up to since he got out. You've been looking into the Moore sisters' background. I'm surprised his name didn't turn up."

"Well, it didn't," Amy said. "I've looked, but there's precious little on either of them."

"In that case you get out there and ask people who knew Agnes and the other one. Come on, Amy, I shouldn't have to tell you how to do your job." Rachel looked at Jonny. "You're with me."

"Suspect is he, this Akerman?" he asked.

"He's a boyfriend of Agnes's and known to have a short fuse. He bought her this." She found the photo and tossed her mobile to him. "We find him, have a chat and go from there. It'll take Amy a little while to get on top of this. Meanwhile, I've asked Stella to email me his record from the system. You look out for it, while I drive."

"Ardwick, at the back of the Apollo. Shouldn't take us long," Jonny said.

Rachel wasn't listening. She was pondering the reason why Anthea hadn't told her about this Akerman bloke. Did the people she worked with know him? They had to, he was from the hostel. She'd sort Akerman and then have another word with both Anthea and Lorraine Hughes at the health centre.

Rachel's mobile beeped. As she was driving, Jonny picked it up. "Info's in. He was done for GBH. Ten years ago. Apparently he beat his wife to a pulp. He didn't bother denying it in court. Too much evidence. He had history. His wife had spent time in a refuge, but she kept going back to him."

Rachel sighed. "Some women never learn."

Minutes later, she pulled up in front of a dingy terraced house.

Jonny cast his eyes over the front of the building. "God, this is the pits."

"Come on, wits about you, this one's got a reputation." Rachel hammered on the door with her fist. "Mr Akerman! Police. We need to speak to you."

No sound from inside. Nothing moved.

"Get round the back," Rachel said. "He might decide to make a run for it."

Rachel called again, and after some time, a man appeared at an upstairs window. "What d'you want?"

"Don Akerman?"

He nodded. Rachel held up her warrant card. "We need to speak to you about Agnes Moore."

He withdrew his head and moments later the front door opened. "Sorry. I'm painting upstairs. I was up a ladder when you knocked."

"Can I come in?" Rachel asked.

He nodded, and she followed him in along a dimly lit hallway. Akerman was tall and thin with a slight stoop. He had dark circles around his eyes and sunken cheeks. Rachel had seen many addicts in her time, and Akerman certainly looked the part.

"I'm doing the place up. Property's booming in Manchester at the moment, and I hope to sell it at a profit," he said.

"When did you last see Agnes?" Rachel asked, unimpressed with this explanation.

"Monday. Before she went away. I met her after work and we had a drink and a bite to eat in the pub."

"Which pub?" she asked.

"The Grapes, opposite the health centre." He looked her up and down. "What's this about? Is Agnes alright?"

Rachel's eyes narrowed. "Why? What d'you know?"

"Nothing," he said. "All I know is that Agnes was going away. We had a chat over a meal and she got a taxi home. That's it."

"Agnes has been murdered," Rachel said bluntly. "Badly beaten and brutally killed, Mr Akerman."

He scowled. "So straight away you come for me. I've got a record, and I'm no saint, but I don't hurt women, not anymore, and I certainly don't kill them."

"You have a pretty damning history though. You did half-kill your wife, and you did time for it," Rachel said.

"I'm a different man now!" he shouted, pushing his face close to hers. "I've got a job at the homeless shelter in Beswick. I manage the place, so don't piss me off with crap about my past."

"Calm down," Rachel said.

"Sorry. I just get het up when that rears its ugly head. But I've changed. Ask anyone. Ask at the hostel, they'll tell you. That's where I met Agnes. We both do our best to help those people."

"I want you to come down to the station with me," said Rachel. She wanted a statement from him about Monday. She also wanted to check out his tale about being in the Grapes.

"Why? Am I under arrest? I've done nowt. You can't make me."

"You're helping us with our enquiries," she said. "I'm sure you want to know who killed Agnes every bit as much as we do."

He sighed. "Give me a minute to lock the back door."

Rachel had forgotten about Jonny. He must still be around the back.

"Mr Akerman!" She ran after him. But the back door was swinging on its hinges. He'd gone. There was no sign of Jonny either.

Rachel swore and made a dash for the yard gate. Pulling it open, she heard Jonny shouting for help. There, in the ginnel at the back of the terrace, he had a kicking and screaming Akerman pinned to the ground.

"Get the cuffs on him," she said. "We're taking him in."

CHAPTER TEN

Rachel was addressing the team. "We have Don Akerman in the cells. As yet we have no evidence to link him to Agnes's murder, but the moment he got the chance, he ran. He's afraid of something, and he has a history of violence against women. So he remains a person of interest until we prove otherwise."

"The attack on his wife was particularly vicious." Amy was reading from the report. "He broke several ribs."

Rachel looked at Jonny. "The Grapes pub in Beswick. Get down there pronto and ask if Akerman was there with Agnes on Monday evening. I want to know what time they arrived and when they left, and if they argued at all." She turned to Amy. "There is CCTV down that road. Have it sent over. You might see them leaving. It's important to discover what Agnes did when she left that pub, and how she got home, if she ever did."

"I eventually got the footage from the bank," Elwyn said. "It won't be long before we see who withdrew that money."

Rachel went to her office. Once she had some feedback from Jonny, she'd interview Akerman. She accessed his record on the system and read through it for herself. Amy was right, he'd been one vicious bastard. Wife beating, and a history of going ballistic. He'd lost jobs in the past because of his short fuse.

"Rachel, you need to see this," Elwyn said.

She followed Elwyn to his desk in the incident room. He had frozen the CCTV at the point where Agnes's debit card was being used.

"He withdrew a hundred quid, no receipt, stuffed the cash in his pocket and legged it."

Rachel looked at the image closely. There was no mistaking who it was. Akerman.

"How did he get hold of her card and the PIN?" Elwyn asked.

"Print out that shot and we'll go and ask him," Rachel said.

"You're not waiting for Jonny?"

Rachel turned to Amy. "Let me have the information as soon as he gets back. Any luck with the CCTV?"

"They're sending me a link to the footage, ma'am," Amy said.

* * *

Rachel and Elwyn went into the interview room. "Mr Akerman, would you like a solicitor?" she asked.

"Do I need one?"

She sat down facing him across the formica table. "I'm DCI King and this is Sergeant Pryce. We want to interview you about your relationship with Agnes Moore, and what happened on Monday evening. Are you happy to continue?"

Immediately he became agitated. "You can't think I had anything to do with her death? I'd never hurt her."

"Well, someone did." This made him squirm. "And they didn't hold back. You have history, Mr Akerman. You beat your wife half to death and went down for it."

The look on his face was poisonous. "I'm not that man anymore, I told you. You people, you never give folk like me the benefit. I loved Agnes. We were planning a future together."

Rachel put down a photograph in front of him. It was the one showing him at the ATM. "What were you doing with her debit card?"

He looked from one detective to the other. "She gave it to me. I was a bit short, see. Agnes said she didn't need it on holiday, she said she'd take her credit card instead."

Rachel leaned forward, a look of disbelief on her face. "You expect me to believe that load of rubbish? You're a real piece of work, aren't you? You stole it from her, didn't you? That's the truth of it."

"No! I told you, she gave it to me."

"How did you get hold of her PIN?" she asked.

"She told me it. Why would I lie?"

"Perhaps because you killed her and thought you'd help yourself. You argued on Monday night, didn't you? Lost your temper and couldn't control it. That's what happened, isn't it?" Rachel said.

"No! No! I would never hurt her."

Elwyn cleared his throat. "So, if you have nothing to hide, why did you run from DCI King and her colleague?"

"I knew that if you brought me in, I wouldn't stand a chance," Akerman said. "I didn't want to go down again, for something I didn't even do."

"You saw Agnes the day she died. How was she?" Elwyn asked.

"We had a drink in the Grapes after she finished work. She was fine. When I left her, she was going home to pack. She'd borrowed a suitcase from a workmate — bloody great thing it was. We joked about the amount of stuff she was taking."

"How did she get home?" Rachel asked.

"She ordered a taxi. I left her outside the Grapes, waiting for it."

"Why didn't you wait with her?" asked Rachel. "It's a rough part of town. Didn't you worry for her safety?"

"She didn't want me to. She works just across the road and knew the score. Anyway, it was raining, so she told me to go. Said she'd be fine."

"Did you hear from her after that?" asked Elwyn.

"She said she'd ring me when she arrived at her hotel."

"Didn't you wonder why that didn't happen, Mr Akerman?" Rachel asked.

He shrugged. "Not really."

"You were fond of Agnes. Isn't that so?" Rachel said.

"Yes, of course I was. We'd got close over the last few weeks."

"So why not ring or text her? Find out how she was after the flight. Make sure she'd made the hotel okay."

"Because, DCI King, she'd had a busy time of it at work and she wanted a week away to rest up." He shook his head. "Agnes hated fuss. I knew she wouldn't want me bothering her every five minutes."

"Not even a quick call or text? You know, check in, make sure she's okay. You say you were close but your apparent lack of concern doesn't reflect that."

Rachel saw the look he gave her. Akerman didn't take criticism well, and, given his history, especially not coming from a woman. "We'll give you some time to think things through," she said. "I suggest you arrange for a solicitor to be present the next time we talk." She stood up and began to gather up her notes.

"You have to believe me. I didn't harm Agnes. She was fine when I left her."

"A uniformed officer will arrange for a solicitor to be present at our next interview."

"Can I go home? I've got work tonight."

"I'm afraid not, Mr Akerman. You haven't answered all my questions yet."

"I don't know what else I can tell you," he said.

"Try the truth, Mr Akerman." Rachel marched out.

Out in the corridor, Elwyn said, "You came on a bit strong there, Rachel. We have no real proof that he's guilty."

"Until we know different, he stays here. The man is a bully and he batters women. He is a prime suspect."

Jude Glover was waiting for them in the incident room. She smiled. "I'm told you're interviewing someone. Quick work."

"Agnes had a boyfriend — a convicted wife batterer, would you believe? Want a coffee?" Rachel said.

"No time, sorry. I'm on my way to a meeting. I popped in to tell you that we've finished examining Agnes's flat and we found something rather interesting. She had a guest. It's a one bedroom apartment but someone had been sleeping on the sofa in the sitting room. And that someone has dyed pink hair."

Rachel immediately recalled the girl who'd approached them. This was just too much of a coincidence.

"Thanks, Jude. As a matter of fact, Elwyn and I met a girl with pink hair outside the health centre where Agnes worked. We'll get on it."

"There was something else — a diary," Jude said. "It looks like she used it for appointments. There are various girls' names against dates, plus the odd address." She handed Rachel an evidence bag containing a small black book.

This was important. "I bet she saw the girls in her own time, possibly at her flat. Thanks. This could be just what we need."

Rachel's phone beeped. It was Jonny.

"Ma'am, I've just had an interesting conversation with the landlord of the Grapes. Agnes Moore and Don Akerman had a heated argument in there Monday. Things got so bad he had to ask them to leave. Outside on the street, Akerman punched her arm. Agnes was visibly upset. The landlord doesn't know where they went but she didn't get into any taxi. Last thing he saw was Agnes trundling down the footpath, dragging a suitcase behind her."

"Thanks, Jonny. What time was this?"

"He reckons it was about five thirty."

Rachel turned to the team. "Akerman was lying. He did have a row with Agnes in the Grapes, and he hit her. Amy, find out if he has a vehicle. I think we should have forensics check it over."

"Email me the details of his home address, Rachel, and we'll get on with it right away," Jude said.

Rachel went to her office to check the PM report. It stated that Agnes had died at about eight that Monday evening. So what happened to her between five thirty and the time she was murdered?

Returning to the incident room, Rachel spoke to one of the uniforms. "Mr Akerman will be staying the night," she said. "Make sure he understands." She checked the time. Next on the agenda was the health centre and that appointment card. Finding the identity of the other young girl was a priority.

"DCI King?"

Rachel spun round to see a uniformed officer standing at the incident room door. He handed her a slip of paper.

"We've had a call from a DS Howe at Salford CID. He asked if you would ring him urgently."

What did he want? She wasn't aware of anything they were currently involved in that would interest Salford.

She turned to Jonny. "Make sure Jude has all the information she needs."

Rachel went to her office and phoned the number on the slip of paper.

"What can I do for you? And make it quick, we're up to our eyes in a murder case," she said.

"We've got your daughter Megan at Salford station. She's asked that you be present when we interview her."

CHAPTER ELEVEN

The DS from Salford had refused to tell her anything over the phone. Keeping this juicy little family titbit to herself and merely telling the team that she had to go out, Rachel drove off. She was bloody annoyed. So much for that chat with Lorraine Hughes. What the hell was Megan up to?

She arrived at Salford and was taken to a soft interview room, where Megan sat drinking coffee. She looked pale, dishevelled, short of sleep and in need of some clean clothes.

"Now what, Megan?" Rachel demanded. "You don't come home for two days, and then you turn up in a police station."

"Don't go on, Mum. It's nothing. They've got it all wrong."

Rachel sat down beside her. "The police don't bring people in for no reason, Megan. What have you been up to?"

The girl averted her eyes. "There was a party," she finally admitted. "I suppose it got a bit out of hand. I think one of the neighbours must have rung this lot."

As Megan spoke, DS Howe and a uniformed officer entered the room. Howe was heavily built and tanned, with short fair hair. He smiled. "Sorry to keep you."

"Look, is this really necessary?" Rachel asked. "I've got a mountain of work back at the office. If it was a lift home she needed, Megan could've rung her dad."

Much to Rachel's annoyance, DS Howe ignored her and turned to Megan, still smiling. "You're not in any trouble. I'm hoping that you can help us. Tell me about last night." He sat down opposite them. "How was the party organised, for example?"

"That was down to Nicu," Megan said. "A tenner and you're in."

"How does word get out about these parties?" Howe asked.

"I know about them because he texts Shannon, my friend. Then we tell anyone who might be interested. Word soon spreads."

"Your friend Shannon and Nicu, are they close?" he asked.

"God no! Any contact is about the parties, nothing else."

"So, if he rings her, Shannon must have Nicu's mobile number, right?"

Megan looked at her mum and then back at DS Howe. "Actually, no. She can't contact him. Each time he texts it's always from a different number."

"And you've never thought that odd?" Rachel asked. She knew exactly why this was and how it worked. Nicu was using burner phones. He didn't want to be traced.

"Mum, please don't go on. It's the parties we're interested in, not Nicu. We just need to know when and where. We've never really thought about why he has so many numbers."

"Do you know this Nicu?" Howe asked. "Have you met him?"

"I've seen him once. He always turns up to let us into the apartment and returns later to collect the money. Some of my friends know him. They reckon he's okay."

"Tell me how these parties work," Howe said.

"Nicu has a contact with an apartment in town. It's one of those in that fancy new block in Spinningfields, the one with the rooftop bar. When it's free, he lets people use it. A tenner each for the night, which is good value, far cheaper than a taxi home. We meet up and have a few drinks, that's all." Megan glanced at her mum. "Nothing heavy — until last night that was."

"What happened?" asked Rachel.

"We were gatecrashed. To begin with, there were about thirty of us. We were having a good time. There was plenty of booze and we chatted until the small hours without having to worry about how to get home."

Rachel was astonished. This Nicu bloke had made a cool three hundred quid out of this stupid lot. Not a great deal of money, but he could be at this every night for all they knew. "Have you done this before?" she asked.

"No, but some of my friends have."

"Mrs King," Howe said. "If you don't mind."

"I do bloody mind! What's she here for? Are you charging her with something? Because if not, I'm taking her home."

"Please let Megan talk, Mrs King. We're hoping she can help us."

The expression on his face said he was doing his best to stay patient. Rachel knew she should calm down, but she was stressed. The tightness in her belly told her that much.

"Do you know Nicu's full name?" Howe asked.

Megan shook her head.

"This mate of yours, Shannon, we will have to speak to her. Can I have her name, address and phone number?"

Megan scribbled them down. "She's a student like me, lives in Stalybridge."

Rachel was astonished that her daughter could be such an idiot. "You go into town, to a party organised by a complete stranger. You're not even sure access to the apartment was got legally. You pay over good money to people you don't know. Are you completely stupid, Megan?"

Megan shrugged. "All my mates were going. There's no need to stress, Mum. It was a party. We drank a lot of booze, fooled around and played music. There were no drugs or anything involved. Until those two idiots turned up, everything was fine."

"The people who gatecrashed the party are known to us," Howe explained to Rachel. "This Nicu she talks about is part of a gang we've been keeping an eye on."

That was all she needed! "What's this one got herself into?" Rachel demanded.

He hesitated, and shook his head. "I'm sorry, but there's a deal of effort been put into this operation already. I can't risk gossip."

"Gossip? Do you know who you're talking to? I'm a DCI, for God's sake." Rachel was blazing. How dare he? "You'd better tell me what you know about these people or I'll have a word with your superiors."

That did the trick. "We suspect Nicu, full name Nicu Bogdan, of being involved in people trafficking, among other things."

Short and simple, it hit the spot. A shocked Rachel turned to her daughter. She'd expected him to tell her they'd been smoking weed or something. "Did you know anything about this?"

"Don't be daft, Mum. How could I?" Megan retorted. "Nicu is just someone the others know."

"He sounds Romanian, is that right?" Rachel asked Howe.

"Romanian father and English mother," he said. "He's lived in both countries during his short life, but he seems to have settled here now."

Rachel decided then and there to find out more about Megan's friends. Her daughter might be eighteen but she needed watching.

"We suspect that the apartment in town is a stopping-off point for the ones being moved on. But we think it's also where he sources likely candidates for other work."

Rachel had a bad feeling in the pit of her stomach. "What sort of *other work*?"

"Look, DCI King, I really shouldn't be talking about this. Can I suggest that if you want to know more, you approach DCI Kenton, the SIO in this case?"

Rachel understood the sergeant's concerns. She wouldn't be overly thrilled if one of her team spouted off about their cases either. Time to quiz Megan herself. "Traffickers bring people in from overseas. Was there anyone at this party who didn't speak English, or looked very out of place, Megan?"

"There was a group of girls, six of them. They were very shy and didn't talk to anyone. They were foreign, Eastern European I think."

"Did you see what happened to them?"

"Some bloke showed them in but he didn't stop. The girls just stood around by themselves, and soon a couple of other blokes turned up. They spoke to the girls, but things can't have gone well because there was a lot of shouting."

"Do you know what about?" Howe asked.

"They all went into another room, so we couldn't hear properly."

Howe leaned forward. "What were they like, these men?"

"Smartly dressed. English, I think. When they arrived, they chatted to us lot for a bit, but it was obvious that they were more interested in the foreign girls. Then they took the girls away. That was when it got noisy. The girls screamed blue murder all the way along the corridor. It was obvious they didn't want to go with these blokes."

DS Howe looked at Rachel. "I'm sorry, DCI King, but I've got a couple more questions to ask."

Rachel nodded.

"Did the men or Nicu mention the names of any of these girls?"

"I didn't hear any names, except Ruby. When Nicu let us into the apartment, he kept asking us about Ruby. Where she was, if we'd seen her, that sort of thing."

"You're sure it was Ruby he was interested in?" asked Howe.

"Yes, but she wasn't with us."

"Do you know Ruby's surname?" Howe asked

"No, I don't know her at all. She's just a tag-along. She hangs out with the crowd we know from the pub near the uni. She turns up sometimes and latches on to the group. All I know about her is that she's not happy with her job and is looking for something else."

"We took photos. Take a look at these, see if she's there."

Megan shook her head. "It's a waste of time, 'cause she wasn't. D'you think I'm stupid?"

"Megan! Remember where you are." Rachel nudged her. "Just look at the photos. The girl might be there. You were bladdered, don't forget."

DS Howe found the images on a laptop on the table. He spun it round so that Megan could see. "Take a look and tell me if you see her."

Sulkily, Megan scanned the screen. "Told you. She's not there. And there's no missing her. Common as muck, she is."

"Thanks, Megan, you've been a great help."

As far as Rachel could see, Megan had been no help at all. "What's so special about this Ruby?" she asked. "There's hundreds of pretty girls. Why look for her in particular?"

"I think we'll find that she's on her own, has no family, few friends and won't be missed," Howe said. "We also believe that she was mixed up with the trafficking gang in some way."

"You're saying she'd escaped from them?"

"It appears so, and they won't give up until she's found. This gang is ruthless. They bring girls into the country and sell them into the sex trade and slavery. That's probably what those foreign girls were there for. They also have another lucrative sideline — hiring young girls, particularly runaways, to work for peanuts in sleazy backstreet clubs." He shook his head. "I'm sure I don't have to spell it out for you, DCI King. You'll already know about the grooming gangs that operate locally."

"Grooming gangs?" Megan exclaimed. "Is that what Nicu is involved in?"

"That's what we suspect," Howe told her. "Should he contact you again, or any of your friends, please be sure to let me know." He handed her a card.

Rachel had heard enough. She needed to have a word with Megan. Her daughter was a bloody liability at times. "Is that it? Can we go now?"

Howe nodded. "If you recall anything else, Megan, contact me."

* * *

As soon as they were outside the station, Rachel tackled her daughter. "Do you realise the danger you were in? It could have been you they targeted. You swan about, trusting complete strangers . . . You can't carry on like that, Megan. It's a dangerous world out there."

"Give it a rest, Mum. Nothing happened, and Ruby will be fine."

"You can't know that. Do you know where she lives?"

Megan shrugged. "No idea. I've never really spoken to her that much, even though she's always around."

"I don't want you staying out all night again. Got it?"

"I'm eighteen," Megan said. "I can please myself."

Rachel groaned. This was going to be some fight. Her daughter was stubborn and independent — both traits she got from her. "While you live under my roof and I keep you fed and clothed, you obey my rules, understand?" *Listen to me!* There were times when Rachel opened her mouth and heard her own mother. She'd not been the perfect teen herself, but she'd always known where to draw the line.

"In that case, I'll stay with Dad, he's cool about me going out."

"He won't be so cool when I tell him what happened."

She'd had enough. Rachel took her mobile from her pocket and rang the station. "Hold the fort, Elwyn. Something's come up at home. I'll see you tomorrow."

"Don't stop working because of me," Megan sneered. "You don't usually let what happens to us interfere."

"Now you're really being stupid. I love my job, but you and Mia have always come first."

"In your dreams!" Megan snapped. "One call from work and you drop us in a heartbeat."

"Save it, Megan. We need to get home anyway. Your dad has a guest coming for tea and he wants us all there."

"Why? Who is it?"

"I'll tell you and Mia once we get home. But you behave, okay? Not a word out of place and mind your manners."

"Ah, a woman," Megan said. "Dad's seeing someone. I worked that out a couple of weeks ago. You must think I'm daft. He's been using the aftershave again, and dressing up."

Rachel hadn't noticed a thing. "Well, I must go around with my eyes closed," she said.

"Because you don't have time for us, simple as that."

They drove the rest of the way in silence. Megan could be a pain in the backside when she chose. But that didn't stop Rachel trying to protect her. The girl had no idea how dangerous Manchester could be.

CHAPTER TWELVE

"Get yourself sorted," Rachel told Megan back at home.

"Do we have to dress up?"

"Neat and tidy will do, and go easy on the make-up."

Rachel spotted Mia's school bag in the hall and went upstairs to her youngest daughter's room. She smiled at her. "We're having tea with your dad. He's got a surprise for us."

Still in her uniform, Mia was doing her homework at her desk. "Do I have to come? Ella's mum said she'd take us for a burger later."

Ella was Mia's best friend, and the two of them were practically inseparable.

"It's a bit special," Rachel said. "There's someone your dad wants us to meet."

"Belinda?"

Rachel rolled her eyes. These kids were something else! "How do you know her name?"

"Megan told me. Meggy reckons she's that woman from the farm shop in the village."

"Bellamy's?"

"She works there, apparently."

"Well, your dad wants us there, sweetie. He's cooking something special. Sorry about Ella, but I'm sure she'll understand."

"Will it be lamb?"

Alan did the best roast lamb ever, with all the trimmings. Rachel laughed. "Probably. He'll be wanting to impress her."

"Okay. Can't miss that, can I? I'll ring Ella and tell her."

Back in the hall, Rachel picked the post up off the table. A load of rubbish mostly, but one envelope caught her eye. Her name and address were handwritten, and inside was a cream and silver invitation card. She was invited to the opening night of a new rooftop bar in a tower block in Spinningfields. Rachel read the address again. The block was one of the new ones Jed McAteer had built. Had the invite come from him? If so, what was his game?

She'd read about the bar in the local paper. It was fast becoming the go-to place for the rich and famous, *the* venue in which to be seen. None of that impressed Rachel, but what did pique her curiosity was why he'd invited her. Surely he knew lots of women who'd jump at the chance. It was unsettling. She didn't want Jed McAteer in her life, not in any capacity. But Rachel was a realist, and she knew that sooner or later he was bound to make contact and want to talk about Mia. This was a conversation she was determined to avoid at all costs. Mia was too young and too happy to be saddled with the truth right now.

In less than an hour, Rachel was showered and ready in a pale green fitted dress, whose colour went well with her red hair. Studying her reflection in the full-length mirror, Rachel wondered if she'd chosen wisely. Elwyn had said she'd put a bit of weight on, but the woman staring back at her from the mirror was stick thin. Missed meals, the stress of the job, it all added up to a metabolism working at full tilt.

But it did mean she could stuff her face without it making a jot of difference, which was something to be grateful for. Alan was a great cook. Whatever he served them tonight, lamb or something else, she knew it would be delicious.

"Mum!" Mia shouted up the stairs. "You ready?"

Rachel stepped into a pair of heels and went to join her girls. "Put this in your pocket for me." She handed Megan her mobile.

Megan rolled her eyes. "Can't you leave it behind for even one meal?"

"No, I can't," Rachel said. "We're dealing with a murder at work and things change fast. I need to be in the loop. And don't turn it off."

Megan replied with a huge yawn.

"You should try spending a few nights at home," Rachel said.

Megan muttered something. "Please don't bring that up. Not tonight."

"What're you talking about?" Mia asked.

"Nothing you need to bother about." Rachel nudged Megan. "My silence costs, young lady. You behave, I keep my mouth shut, okay?"

"Agreed, but please don't leave us alone with dad and his girlfriend. I'm having a hard enough time staying awake as it is."

"You're one cheeky brat, aren't you?" Rachel grinned. "We'll eat, make some friendly small talk and then leave them to it. And no smart remarks. Your dad will be as nervous as hell, so go easy on him. Got that?"

There was a white sports car parked on Alan's drive. Rachel eyed the gleaming paintwork. "Works in the farm shop, you said. You sure about that?"

"She's served me in there more than once," Mia said.

"Well you don't buy one of those on a shop-worker's wages."

Alan greeted her with the usual kiss on the cheek and ushered the three of them inside."

"This is okay? You've nothing else on?"

Rachel shook her head.

"I had Ade round today. He's still on about the extension," Alan said.

"Thought we'd shelved that one," Rachel said.

"We have — that's if you don't mind. It suits me to leave things as they are for now."

"I was never keen in the first place. Too much money and upheaval."

They were still standing in the hallway. Rachel smiled. "Can we come through then, and meet your guest?"

"Sorry. I'm a bit nervous. I want this to go right. It means a lot."

Rachel patted his arm. "Stop stressing, we're all fine."

He really was twitchy. This woman must be important.

"Homework done?" Alan asked Mia. "Finished that tricky bit?"

"Yeah, Dad, everything's cool."

"Megan?"

"Calm down," Rachel said. "We're not going to rock the boat. Get me a drink and introduce us."

The three of them followed him into the sitting room. Belinda was standing at the window, looking out at the back garden.

She turned and smiled. "Lovely views you've got from here."

Rachel couldn't recall seeing her before. Mind you, she hardly ever shopped locally. "Yes, we're very lucky." She stuck out her hand. "I'm Rachel and these are the kids, Megan and Mia. Nice to meet you." She smiled.

"And you too. I'm surprised we haven't met before now. I have the shop, the farm, and I'm also involved in a lot of stuff locally."

Rachel suddenly realised who this woman was — Belinda Bellamy. Her family owned the farm up in the hills above Poynton. Over the years, they had turned the place into a thriving business. They were well-known locally, and had to be worth a fortune.

"It's my job, Belinda," Rachel explained. "It takes up all of my time and then some."

"A bit like mine." Belinda laughed. "Getting up at the crack of dawn to milk the cows is no fun, believe me."

Rachel shuddered inwardly. She couldn't think of anything worse, particularly on icy winter mornings. Belinda seemed nice enough, but no great beauty. She was plump. Her blonde hair hung in dishevelled waves around her face. She wasn't wearing any make-up and her clothes were old. She was nothing like the sort of woman Rachel had imagined Alan going for.

He appeared in the doorway. "I've done lamb. It's from Belinda's shop. She reared the animal herself."

"Lambing was good this year," Belinda said. "All our ewes produced. I picked this one specially for tonight."

"Do you do the slaughtering yourselves?" Rachel asked rather tentatively.

"Yes, we're all kitted out. The meat we sell is all home-grown and forms a large part of our business. I did that one myself."

Poor lamb, thought Rachel and wondered if she'd be able to actually eat the creature. Images of the little thing running and jumping around the fields mingled with ones of Belinda catching and butchering the beast.

"Haven't you ever been married?" Rachel asked.

"I almost did, many years ago, but he got on the wrong side of my father. Chased him off with a shotgun he did, bless him." This was said rather wistfully, whether for the suitor or the dad Rachel wasn't quite sure. "He was a cantankerous old sod, but I still miss him."

"You run the farm on your own?" Rachel asked.

"I'm an only child, so yes. What'll happen when I can't manage it anymore is anyone's guess. I'm a little old now to produce offspring."

Rachel hoped she meant that, and wasn't looking at Alan as father material. He'd had the snip years ago. Rachel wondered if he'd told Belinda.

"You lost your parents too, Alan tells me," Belinda said.

75

Rachel took a slug of the wine Alan handed her. This wasn't something she usually spoke about. "They were both killed in a car crash a couple of years ago. It was a devastating time. I miss them a lot."

The conversation was taking a bad turn. She was saved by her mobile ringing in Megan's pocket.

A scowling Megan handed it over and Rachel went into the hallway to take Elwyn's call.

"Amy's spotted something important on the CCTV from Ashton Old Road," he began. "Agnes is clearly seen outside the Grapes, walking away from Akerman and dragging the suitcase behind her. Akerman remains outside the pub, watching her. He looks angry, but he doesn't give chase. He waits a few minutes and then walks off in the opposite direction. We then picked Agnes up a few metres further on. She is talking to someone in a white van that pulled up beside her. The van drives away but there is no longer any sign of Agnes."

"Did you see where she went?"

"The CCTV quality is poor and it was raining. It looks like the driver pulled her in on the side of the van that's away from the camera. The suitcase was left on the pavement."

Rachel had a bad feeling. Elwyn could be right. "What did Akerman do?"

"We pick him up further down the road, still going in the opposite direction. He goes into a kebab shop and spends a good fifteen minutes talking to the bloke in there. Whoever picked Agnes up, it wasn't him."

Rachel had been so sure Akerman was their killer. "Did you get the registration?"

"Yes, already checked it out. It's fake."

"Damn! Get the images of that van printed, and see if you can pick it up again. We need to know where that van went, Elwyn."

CHAPTER THIRTEEN

Day Three

The team gathered in the incident room early the following morning. Rachel had already studied the CCTV and satisfied herself that the information it yielded was limited, but it did appear to rule out Akerman.

"I'll speak to Akerman again," she said. "Despite what I've just watched, I still want an alibi for the time between when he left Agnes and her body being found on that building site. A few minutes buying a kebab isn't good enough. He was close to Agnes. He will know things about her life that we'll find useful." She looked at Jonny. "Do we know who McAteer bought that site from yet?"

"The shops belonged to a company called 'Lion Industrial.' They were all rented out. There have been a variety of different tenants over the years," Jonny said.

"Who owns this Lion Industrial?"

"It was quite hard to work out. The company has a list of directors as long as your arm, and they've all come and gone, except for a man called Ronan Blake. He is also down as being the person the shopkeepers and tenants in the flats paid their rent to."

Rachel frowned. The name was familiar, but she couldn't think where from. "Has he been involved for a while?" she asked.

"He has been a Lion director for twenty years."

Rachel nodded. "More research, Jonny. I want the names of all the people who've had an interest in that company. I've nothing to back it up, but I have a gut feeling that there's a link between that site and the deaths of our unknown female and Agnes. It's vital that we find the identity of our unknown." Rachel looked at Amy. "She was two months dead and had given birth. Agnes was a nurse, who helped people in need. A young girl asked Elwyn and I about Agnes on the street outside the health centre. She was wearing similar clothing to that of our unknown. Have you discovered anything else about Agnes that might help us?"

Amy shook her head. "She appears to have been just an ordinary woman."

"I doubt there's any such thing," Rachel said. "You and Jonny get back there. Knock on a few doors around the centre. Go round the shops and find out who the young girl with the pink hair is. Shouldn't be too hard. With hair like that, she couldn't pass unnoticed." She turned to Jonny. "Do we know what Ronan Blake is up to now?" He shook his head. "Find out. Get a full background and we'll pay him a visit."

"What about Akerman?" Elwyn asked. "Looks like he was telling the truth."

"Even so, the man bothers me. I still have the feeling that he knows more than he's telling us. We'll interview him again. See if a night in the cells has softened him up."

* * *

Don Akerman wasn't happy. When the detectives entered the interview room, he was pacing up and down, his fists clenched. As soon as he saw them, he yelled, "I want out! You've no right to keep me here. I've done nowt."

"Very soon," Rachel said. "Meanwhile, I need you to tell me about Agnes. What sort of woman was she?"

On hearing the name, he stopped pacing and sat down. After a pause, he said quietly, "She was kind. Always happy to give folk the benefit. She took me on." He looked away, embarrassed. "I'm no catch, and Agnes had a lot going for her."

"She helped people from the hostel," Rachel said, "including some young women. Do you know where they came from?"

He looked from one detective to the other, apparently unsure of what to say. "They were patients, I think. She even had one of them sleeping on her couch. Poor kid had nowhere to go."

He knew more, Rachel was sure of it. "Do you know where this girl worked?"

"Some place in town, a bar, I think. Agnes went down there one night. Took them to task about conditions." He lowered his eyes. "She reckoned the owner wasn't paying enough, and she was worried about their lack of freedom."

"What d'you mean, lack of freedom?" Elwyn asked.

"They worked and lived at that club, and rarely went anywhere else."

"Do you know the names of any of these girls?" Rachel asked.

He shrugged. "No idea."

Rachel stiffened. "Are you sure?"

"Told you, didn't I?"

Rachel wondered if the girl who'd slept on Agnes's sofa was the one DS Howe was looking for. "And the bar?"

"I've no idea, just some back street boozer." He looked away. "Worked the poor kids like slaves and paid peanuts. Agnes got herself proper worked up about it."

"Mr Akerman, are you sure you don't know where this boozer is?"

He shook his head. "Agnes didn't tell me everything. Anyway, it doesn't do to rub folk up the wrong way."

That was an odd thing to say. "Did someone threaten you?"

He smiled. "No. Why would anyone do that? I'm nobody."

"What did you do when you left that kebab shop?" Elwyn asked.

"I went home. Well, I had nothing better on, had I? Bert was waiting for me. He lives in the flat above. We played cards and drank some cans. It must have been gone midnight when he left."

Rachel made a mental note to have that checked. "Can I have his full name, please?"

"Bert Madden. Ask anyone, they'll show you his place."

* * *

They made their way back to the incident room.

"Not him then," Elwyn said.

Rachel was disappointed. "And there was me thinking we'd got it wrapped up. Akerman appeared to be the perfect candidate for Agnes." She heaved a sigh. They'd put in a lot of work and got nowhere. "But he is afraid of someone. We need to identify that poor girl and quick, before Harding starts breathing down our necks. And we need to find the name and address of that bar." She dumped the interview paperwork on the nearest desk. "Did you know that Salford are investigating a people trafficking and grooming ring?"

"No, but it doesn't surprise me," Elwyn said.

"It surprised me. We've heard nothing our end. It could be big. And if it is, it won't stay Salford's side of the Irwell. I wonder if this is what we've got on our hands? The girls, their lack of freedom, the fact that they seem to run whenever the opportunity presents itself. And we've got a body."

Elwyn looked dubious. "We've enough on our plates. Let's not go looking for trouble."

"Good advice," Rachel said, "but we can't ignore what's staring us in the face. For now, we'll keep an open mind. And there is something else."

Rachel went into her office and beckoned Elwyn to follow. "Megan got herself involved in a party scam the other night. Some bright spark hires out a fancy town apartment to the kids at a tenner each for the night. They think it's great. No expensive taxi home to pay for. The party was gatecrashed by a couple of blokes no one knew. There was a group of foreign girls there too, possibly trafficked. Megan was no help on that score. It got noisy and the police were called. A DS Howe from Salford interviewed Megan about who she saw there. Despite everything else that was going on, he was particularly interested in a missing girl called Ruby."

Elwyn frowned. "Your daughter needs to be careful. That sounds like heavy stuff she's stumbled into."

"Don't worry, Elwyn, I'll be having a word. But don't you see? That's what both our unknown and our runner could be part of."

CHAPTER FOURTEEN

Lorraine Hughes wasn't pleased to see the two detectives. "I told the other one everything I know." She sighed. "Look, I'm sorry about Agnes but I've nothing to add."

"We're not here about Agnes," Jonny said. "What d'you know about a young woman with pink hair?"

Lorraine Hughes folded her arms. "Oh, her. She was one of Agnes's hopeless cases. There were a few, came here looking for God knows what, and expecting Agnes to sort it. That one, the one with the hair, she was trouble. Baggage, if you know what I mean."

"No, we don't. Enlighten us, Ms Hughes," Jonny said with some sarcasm. *Baggage.* Sounded positively Victorian.

"She was always on edge. I reckon she's an addict. Came here to score drugs. Of course, Agnes wouldn't have any of that."

"Do you have any records — a name? Address?" Amy asked her.

She frowned. "I'm not sure. I shouldn't think so. They were Agnes's project. Mostly the girls just wanted to talk. They were cagey about names and addresses, most wouldn't even register as temporaries. Agnes took the view that they needed help and should get it regardless. Not ideal. It does nothing for our funding."

"Are you sure about the records, Ms Hughes?" Jonny said. "We can easily get a warrant, come back mob-handed and search the entire premises. We'd prefer not to have to do it. We have no desire to worry your patients."

"No need for that. Like I said, it was advice they wanted. A cup of tea, a few kind words and they went on their way." She shrugged.

"How many did she see, do you know?" Amy asked.

"Lately it was mostly the girl with the pink hair. And there was another one. Scared of her own shadow, she was. There were others before them. The faces change so frequently, it's hard to keep up," Lorraine Hughes said dismissively. "Agnes was a right soft touch. You'd be better off asking at the hostel. They sometimes went there for a bite to eat."

"Do you recognise this?" Jonny showed her a copy of the appointment card found underneath the unknown girl.

Lorraine Hughes squinted at it briefly. "I can barely see it. It could be anything."

"We think it's an appointment card for here. If it is, then this girl was registered as a patient. It's roughly two months old and the girl was pregnant. Would you check, please? If it is for an appointment here, there should be a record."

"But you can't read it, the name is obliterated. There's nothing to go by," Lorraine said.

"We'd appreciate it if you'd give it a go. A young pregnant girl, possibly booked in to see Agnes," Amy said. "Otherwise, like DC Farrell says, it'll be the warrant and a shedload of upheaval."

Lorraine Hughes rolled her eyes. "We'll try, but our time is limited."

"Do your best. I'll leave this with you." Amy handed over her card. "Give me a ring when you've got something."

Leaving a visibly disgruntled Lorraine, they went outside.

"Shall we walk? The hostel is only up the road," Jonny said. "We can ask at the shops on the way."

Amy cast a wary eye up the road. "This is a rough part of town. Don't be surprised if we get told to piss off."

They first tried the newsagents, where the woman behind the counter, chewing slowly on a piece of gum, eyed them with suspicion. "Who wants to know?"

"We're police." Jonny showed her his warrant card. "Do you know the girl I've described?"

"Pink hair, you say." She blew a bubble. "Might do. In fact, she might have been round here yesterday."

"Do you know her name?" asked Amy.

"I serve 'em fags and stuff. I take the cash and that's it. I don't get paid for idle chitchat." She frowned, as if recalling something. "There was some bloke came in here, looking for her. He stood behind that display unit by the window and watched folk walk past. She came out of the health centre and he was after her like a shot."

"D'you know who he was?"

"No. I've said enough. It doesn't do to be seen talking to t'police round 'ere."

"Do you know him?" Amy was fed up of getting nowhere. "Obstructing enquiries is an offence."

The woman blew another bubble. It popped loudly. "Can't tell you what I don't know, and no amount of bullying from you lot will change that."

Reluctantly, Jonny and Amy left and walked on up the road. After a few minutes, Amy said, "She knew that bloke. It was written all over her face. What is it with people? We're dealing with cold blooded murder here."

"I've just had a text from DCI King," Jonny said, ignoring her rant. "They got nothing from Akerman. They asked about the girl and got nowhere. He reckons he doesn't know her."

Amy sighed. "It's down to us then."

The hostel came into view and Jonny groaned. Once again, there was a fight. Two men were rolling around on the pavement, and one of the men was taking a right beating.

"They do nothing but fight in this place," complained Jonny.

"Well, we'll have to do something." Leaving Jonny behind, Amy ran forward, screaming, "Police!" and flashing her warrant. She tugged at an arm. "Get off him!"

"Leave 'em, love. That pair's been at each other's throats all day, and it'll be the same tomorrow." Mavis Smithson stood, arms folded, in the doorway of the hostel.

"What's the argument about?" Jonny asked.

She shrugged. "They're off their faces, so who knows?"

The smaller of the two men rolled into the gutter, lay still for a few seconds and then got to his feet and staggered off, swearing.

"What d'you want?" Mavis asked the detectives. "Only you'd better not come in. The lot of them in there are fired up and itching for a fight."

"We're looking for a girl with pink hair," Amy said. "Does she come here?"

"That sounds like Ruby. Yeah, she visits from time to time. She's usually looking for Don."

Ruby. At last they had a name.

"Why, what's their connection?" Amy asked.

Mavis waved her hand vaguely. "No use asking me, love. I don't get involved. They're usually okay — get things sorted because of what Agnes does for them — but last time she was here, Don and her had a row. Left in a right strop she did. Come to think about it, we've not seen her since."

Amy looked at Jonny. "We need to get back. We have a name — Ruby, and Akerman knew her. We should tell the boss. He lied to her."

* * *

It was late afternoon. The school was empty, the noise of the working day long gone and no prying eyes to watch his progress along the dimly lit corridors. Every inch of this dump was familiar to him. He'd spent the last two years of his schooldays here. The place should have been torn down years ago. The promises kept coming, but the new build never materialised. He knew exactly where to find *her* too. Both this place and the woman he'd come to see were unhappy reminders of his past.

She was seated at her desk, head down, intent on the pile of exercise books in front of her. A curtain of grey-brown hair fell over her face, obliterating her view of the doorway. For a moment, he was back there again. The bad old days and this woman, red-cheeked, lips flecked with spittle, flying at him in a rage. His sins were legion, and top of the list was the way he intimidated the younger element in the school. Over the years, his talent for bullying had made him a fortune.

Seeing her now, he couldn't believe she'd ever scared him. There had been times when she'd frightened him even more than his waster of a father. Look at her. She was nothing special. She was just an ordinary woman, ageing and ready for retirement. As he walked closer, she gave a 'tut' of disapproval and swiped that red pen of hers over an entire page. He pitied the poor kid who'd written the piece. Stupid bitch! Who did she think she was?

"You!"

She'd seen him. Not only that but she'd recognised him as well. He was flattered. He smiled. Best not alarm her. "Things don't change, do they?" He spun around, waving his hand at the flaky paintwork and tall, vaulted ceiling. "Freezing in winter, these rooms. None of the windows fit properly. The whole lot should be condemned. You oughter complain, Miss Moore. It's not fair, teaching kids in these conditions."

She regarded him with small, dark eyes. After a lengthy silence, she said, "The new school is nearly finished. The handover is scheduled for next term." She stared at him. "Surely you're not a parent?"

He heard the derision, but smiled all the same. She'd inadvertently given him a way in. He shook his head. "No. Concerned older brother."

"One of mine, is he? Or is it a she?"

"She." He paused. "I'm worried that she's not getting enough encouragement. It'll be GCSEs next and I don't think she's ready. She gets worried, panics, you know how it is. We can't keep her at home. The silly girl keeps running away."

She reached for the register. "Name?"

Short and not so sweet. Nothing had changed. "Ruby Bogdan," he said.

"I don't recall her. Are you sure she's one of mine?"

"Yes, I'm certain. You might know her as Ruby Wood. Sometimes she uses our English grandmother's name."

The woman's face clouded with suspicion. "I know her alright. You say she's your sister?" Her voice was laden with doubt. "Are you sure, Nicu? She's never mentioned you."

He grinned. "Wouldn't, would she? Our Rubes knows my reputation. When did you see her last?"

"Since you're not her guardian, I'm afraid I can't discuss Ruby with you. Get a parent to come in and talk to me."

"No parents. There's only me. Look, if you know where she is, you have to tell me."

"Can't help, Nicu. Ruby isn't here, that's all I can say."

He moved closer. "If she turns up, you'd do well to tell me. I'd hate to see you get hurt."

The teacher's eyes widened. "Are you threatening me, Bogdan? How dare you! You insolent, little . . ."

His laughter echoed around the room. "Ain't that the truth." Suddenly the laughter became a scowl and he slammed a fist down on her desk. "Where's she hiding? Is she with one of those stupid friends of hers? Tell me now, bitch, and you'll save yourself a deal of aggro."

She got to her feet. "Get out of here or I'll call security."

Another laugh. "That stupid old goat won't even hear you. You're a joke, you and this place."

"I warn you, I'll ring the police."

Nicu held up his hands. "Okay, but be sure to tell Ruby I'm looking for her. She knows what happens to girls who run out on the boss."

CHAPTER FIFTEEN

"I knew he was lying!" Rachel said. She smiled at Amy. "Good work. We'll speak to Akerman again, ask him why he didn't tell us the girl's name in the first place."

"He may have been keeping it secret because of Agnes. We have no idea what kind of relationship she had with the other girls," Elwyn said.

"You're right, Elwyn. Amy, ask the health centre if Ruby was a patient there," Rachel said.

"I've got them looking for the dead girl too," Amy said. "There's not much to go on, but who knows? Oh, and I've got the CCTV through from the building site." She smiled. "They took their time but it was worth the wait. The only vehicle to visit the site that evening was a white van."

Rachel recalled the footage of the van stopping beside Agnes that night. Same one? Had to be, it was too much of a coincidence. "Print out a series of stills and I'll have a look when we come back."

"Okay, ma'am, I'll do that and leave the report on your desk."

Amy was showing promise again. The young DC could be bone idle until something motivated her. If only she was more consistent.

"You drive, Elwyn," Rachel said. "I need to ring home, check on those kids. The name Ruby came up when that sergeant from Salford interviewed Megan. The girl knows her. Ruby hangs out with them occasionally."

"Sails a bit close to the wind, your daughter. She needs to be careful."

"Don't worry, I'm on it." While the house phone rang, Rachel regarded her colleague. Would he be interested in what she was about to suggest? "I don't want you to take this the wrong way but I'm short of a plus one for an event. I wondered if you . . ."

His eyes widened. "You're inviting me out?"

He remained staring at her while Megan answered her call.

"You both okay?" Rachel asked.

"Fine, and Dad's doing tea."

"Well, don't leave the house. You and me need a serious chat. I've got a few questions for you." Rachel waited for the inevitable protest.

Megan didn't disappoint. "I've got a date tonight. What do I tell him, that I'm grounded? I'm eighteen for God's sake!"

"You stay put until I get home." Rachel ended the call and turned to Elwyn.

"It's not a date or anything," she added hastily. "It might even be work, I'm not sure."

"Go on then, explain."

"I've been invited to a posh drinks do tomorrow evening. It's at the rooftop bar of that new apartment block in Spinningfields. I don't want to go on my own, so I thought of you." She smiled at him.

He chuckled. "Only because there's no one else."

How true that was. Rachel didn't like to think about it, but other than her immediate family and work colleagues, she had no one in her life.

"Look, don't mess me around. Are you in or not?" she said.

"Why not ask Alan?"

"He's got a new woman and I think it might be serious. I don't want to cause any ill feeling. She probably thinks we're weird as it is, living next door and cooking each other meals."

"How come you've been invited?" Elwyn asked.

"The apartments have something to do with Jed. Another reason why I don't want to go alone," Rachel said. "If I do, he'll just get the wrong idea."

"So why go at all, why not just cry off?"

"Because that party Megan went to was held in an apartment in the same block. I thought I'd take a look at the people who own them. Given the Ruby connection, it might be useful."

She saw the look. Elwyn was sceptical. It didn't matter what she said, he thought she wanted to go because of Jed McAteer.

* * *

They pulled up in front of Don Akerman's place at the back of the Apollo in Ardwick. The area was rundown, awaiting redevelopment. There were empty houses on the opposite side of the street and a burnt-out car stood centre stage of what passed as a play area at the far end.

"Perhaps we should have brought back-up," Elwyn remarked.

"We're fine. Look around, there's no one here," Rachel said. "This is his — number five." She looked up. The front of the house looked shabby. One of the windows on the upper floor was boarded up and graffiti adorned most of the gable end of the terrace.

The pavement outside was no better. Litter, mostly empty cans and food wrappers, was strewn across it. Stepping gingerly over a discarded pizza carton, Elwyn said, "I suppose it's better than living rough."

"Something's wrong." Rachel stood still for a moment and looked up and down the street, suddenly aware of the eerie silence. "I've been here before with Jonny and it wasn't this quiet. A place like this, I'd expect music, kids knocking about. There's nothing, no one, Elwyn. Why is that?"

"Everyone's at work, or in the pub," he suggested.

"No, look." She pointed at Akerman's house. "There's blood on the pavement over there." She went over and looked down at the smudged rusty mark on the tarmac in front of Akerman's front door, which was slightly ajar. The lock had been smashed and there was an impressive looking boot print on the wood. "Someone's beaten us to it. Gloves on," she said, pulling hers from her pocket. "I've got a bad feeling about this, Elwyn."

Rachel's stomach was churning. This was all wrong. The silent street, the absence of people . . . she pictured the tenants in the other houses all cowering behind their curtains. "We'll have to speak to everyone living along this road. Someone must have seen something."

They stepped inside warily, through a small square hallway and on into the sitting room. There wasn't much in the way of furniture, just the essentials. But they didn't notice the décor. Their eyes had immediately been drawn to the horrific sight in the centre of the room.

Don Akerman was bound to a wooden chair. His head drooped almost to his chest, his wrists attached to the chair arms keeping him from slumping even further forward. His mouth had been gaffer-taped shut and what was left of his face was coated in blood. As Rachel moved closer, she spotted several teeth on the floor. These, more than anything else, made her shudder with revulsion.

Elwyn circled the body and felt the carotid artery for a pulse. "Dead. A bullet to the back of the head."

"Poor man, he's been tortured." Rachel's voice shook. "Look at his hands. They've been screwed down to the wooden chair arms." The brutality of what had been done to him shocked her deeply. She took a breath. "Look at the way his legs are positioned. It's as if someone took a hard object and used it to break as many bones as they could."

91

"What were they after?" Elwyn looked around the poky room. "He's got nothing."

"Information, Elwyn. He knew things. He didn't tell us the half of it." Rachel shook herself. "I need to get the works down here."

"Poor bugger must've suffered. Whoever did this is a right nasty piece of work."

Rachel wasn't listening. Having rung both the incident room and Butterfield, she was now talking to Jude. "There's a good chance of forensics. A patch of blood on the floor looks like it's got a print. Plus, there are boot marks on the door. I need you to come and look at the scene right away. This one is truly bad."

CHAPTER SIXTEEN

Within the hour, Don Akerman's flat was full of white-suited scenes of crime officers, led by Judith Glover. After an initial examination, Butterfield had removed the body to the morgue.

"His hands were very bloody and damaged, so it's difficult to tell if he put up a fight or not, but I doubt he had time. I noticed vomit in his nose and behind the tape," Jude told Rachel. "He was one terrified man."

"I interviewed him earlier today," Rachel said with a frown. "Wish I'd held onto him now."

"You weren't to know," Jude said. "The beating, the brutal way he was killed, he was a man with secrets and he wasn't disclosing them, not even to you."

Rachel shook her head. "I should've put more pressure on him."

"He had pressure here alright, Rachel, extreme pressure. You couldn't even begin to compete." Jude looked at the notes of her initial findings. "From the way his legs were positioned, I'd say both were broken. In my opinion he was beaten with a heavy object. A drill was used to make the holes through his hands and into the chair arms, and then they were screwed in place." Jude Glover looked around the room. "Have you touched anything?"

"Of course not," Rachel said. "Why?"

"That small table by the door is on its side and the lamp is lying on the floor. I think your victim heard the boot at his door, stopped whatever he was doing, moved towards it and was immediately set upon by his killer. The killer grabbed him and slammed him into that chair. There's no carpet, just cheap lino, see?" Jude pointed. "Drag marks."

"In that case, the killer must've been a darn sight stronger than Akerman," Elwyn said.

"Do you have any idea what he was after?" Jude asked.

"Not a clue. I'm trying to see a connection with what happened to Agnes. They were both shot, but her murder was nothing like this. Will you make sure this place gets searched? Top to bottom, under the floorboards, the lot."

Jude nodded. "The boot print on the door is probably the killer's work too. The blood on the floor . . . We'll take a good look around, inside and out. There's blood all over the place. The killer picked some up on his footwear. The prints might just tell us which way he left. I'll get the CCTV sorted too. It's not the nicest part of the city, but there's bound to be something here."

"If you get anything at all, let me know at once," Rachel said.

Jude nodded. "He was brutal but careful, no fingerprints so far, but we'll work on it. You never know. I'll phone you."

Rachel handed Elwyn the car keys. She felt shaky, partly with shock at seeing Akerman's broken body and partly from guilt at letting him walk into this. The violence was over the top. What had he known that was so dangerous it got him killed? Granted, he was a rough diamond. He knew some dodgy people but he'd known Agnes too, and she'd been a good woman.

They drove in silence for a while, until Elwyn said, "This isn't our fault, Rachel. Akerman should have told us what he knew. He must have been aware that the people who killed him were out there, waiting for him. Whatever he was hiding got him killed, not us."

"We let him go. I should have found something to charge him with."

Elwyn shook his head. "What, for God's sake? We had no proof of any wrongdoing."

They fell silent. Rachel was in no mood to debate the matter any further.

* * *

On entering the incident room, they were met by DCS Harding, DS Howe and a man Rachel didn't recognise.

"This is DCI Mark Kenton from Salford Serious Crime squad," Harding said.

Kenton was tall, wiry, his dark hair cut to the bone. His face had a hard, chiselled look. If he hadn't been introduced as a detective, she would have put him down as a thug.

"You've already met DS Colin Howe, I believe," Harding added.

"What's this about?" Rachel was puzzled and a little worried. She thought immediately of Megan.

"The Akerman murder," DCI Kenton said. "We'll be dealing with the case from now on."

Immediately Rachel's hackles were up. Who did he think he was, coming to her nick and laying down the law? She stood facing him, hands on hips. "I beg your pardon? Akerman was killed on our patch. His death is connected to another murder we're investigating." She shook her head. "If you think I'm just going to walk away and let you take over, DCI Kenton, you're very much mistaken."

"You have no choice, and you'd better not cross me on this. We are investigating a number of murders that used exactly the same MO as Akerman's. The fact that the killer has strayed onto your patch is immaterial." He regarded her for a moment, as if choosing his next words carefully. "Sorry, but the case is ours. Might be difficult to swallow, but live with it." He gave her a forced smile. "DCS Harding will back me up. You, lady, are off the case."

She bristled. "Kindly don't refer to me as *lady*. I'm DCI King."

"I'm afraid there is little I can do," Harding said, practically wringing his hands. "The order's come from up above. Please ensure that DCI Kenton has access to all the reports and statements connected with your current case."

Rachel had heard enough. This moron Kenton turns up, and Harding rolls over and does exactly what he's told. She turned on her heel and stormed out. Damn the lot of them! How could Harding stand there and not stick up for his own people? What had happened to the man? He used to be so full of anger that no one dared cross him, but he was showing none of that now. He was fast becoming a pussycat, a leader who allowed his people to walk all over him.

Within minutes, Elwyn was knocking on her office door. "They've gone."

"Bloody piss artists, the lot of them! I won't be bullied off my own case." She looked at Elwyn. "What do we know about this Kenton bloke?"

"He's good, apparently. Another rising star, a bit like yourself."

"He's nothing like me," she retorted. "Whatever he's achieved it'll be by stamping on other officers' toes!"

"We don't know what's going on, Rachel. Who knows? Kenton may have a point."

"DS Howe told me they were investigating a people-smuggling ring with sidelines, and that Ruby was involved with them. Agnes knew her and so, I presume, did Akerman. He told us that a kid had been sleeping at Agnes's. Jude found a pink hair on the sofa if you remember."

"You reckon that whoever did for Akerman was looking for Ruby?"

"Yes, I do, though it's anyone's guess why." Rachel checked the time on her mobile. "I'm going home to have a word with Megan shortly. She's met this Ruby. But first I'm going back to the health centre. I want the record of our young victim's appointment found, and quick. If Harding asks where I am, tell him to bugger off."

CHAPTER SEVENTEEN

"You're wasting your time coming back here again. I've told you everything I know." Lorraine Hughes folded her arms.

Ignoring this, Rachel said, "You were told to check an appointment. A pregnant or newly delivered young woman. The appointment will have been at least two months ago. What progress have you made?"

"None at all. We're not here to run around after you people. We're a busy practice. My staff work flat out." She regarded Rachel's stony face. "We will get round to it," she said in a softer tone. "We just need time."

Not good enough, especially in Rachel's present mood. "Can I remind you that refusing my request is tantamount to hindering an investigation, and that it carries serious penalties."

"Resorting to threats won't get the job done any quicker." Lorraine Hughes stuck her nose in the air. "There's no pleasing some people. But in the interests of a quiet life, I'll get one of our girls on the job. We have a part-timer comes on after college, she can take a look."

"It's urgent. I won't stand for any further delay. I want this done now."

"Okay, you win." Lorraine Hughes raised her hands. "Have a word with Mary at reception, see if she can do anything for you."

Rachel watched her sashay along the corridor. She was a piece of work. Lorraine Hughes didn't give a damn about what had happened to Agnes, or the young girl.

Rachel went to the reception desk. "Mary? I'm DCI King from East Manchester Serious Crime. I'm investigating the suspicious death of a young girl. She died about two months ago, and she'd given birth. One of your appointment cards was found with the body."

Mary visibly cringed. "Do you have her name?"

"No, sorry, we've no idea who she is."

"Without a name to go on, it will be tricky," she said.

"Couldn't you hive off the pregnant patients under a certain age and go from there?"

"I'll give it a go." Mary busied herself at the computer for a few moments. "That was a good call of yours. We had twelve full-term pregnancies at that time. Three of them were girls under eighteen. They're the ones Agnes was most likely to get involved with."

"Why was that?" Rachel asked.

"She tried to help them, find them a place to live. Some of them would have been living rough."

"They may have given their address as here, or perhaps the hostel. Could you check, please?" Rachel said.

"Do you know if any of them are still patients here?" asked the receptionist.

"I've no idea."

"I'm sorry, I can't find anything. I can give you the names of three girls. At the time, their addresses were given as the hostel up the road. They've probably moved on, hopefully sorted themselves out."

"Did they all have their babies?" Rachel asked.

"The records don't say. But they were all in the final trimester."

"Okay," Rachel said. "Give me the names and I'll check them out."

The receptionist looked doubtful. "Did Mrs Hughes say it was okay?"

Rachel nodded. She didn't give a toss what Lorraine Hughes said.

Rachel went outside and rang Elwyn. "The health centre had three pregnant patients that were close to delivery two months ago. All of them are now off the radar. But they are in the right age range. I've got their names and addresses — not that they're much help. They all gave the hostel as their current residence. They might have known our unidentified girl. I'll text you the names. See if there's anything on the system and report back. And don't say anything to Harding." Kenton could do his own bloody research.

* * *

Rachel left the centre and went home to speak to her daughter. Megan was in her room, busy on her laptop. Rachel could hear her laughing.

"Megan, I need a chat!" she called up the stairs.

"Down in a minute," Megan said.

Rachel put the coffee on. It was a long shot, but Megan might be able to help. Apart from their unknown, she wanted to find Ruby.

"What's brought you home at this hour of the afternoon? Are you ill?" Megan said sarcastically.

"I'm fine, thanks. I want a word with you about that night you spent in Manchester and the people you met, particularly Ruby."

"Told you, she wasn't there. Weren't you listening?" Megan helped herself to a mug of coffee. "What's the interest in her anyway? What's she done?"

"I think she's in danger. I believe some very nasty people are trying to find her. Better we catch up with her first. We've already got one dead girl and we don't want another."

100

Megan's expression became serious. "Ruby's a bit 'out there' — you know, dresses a bit wild, likes a good time. But she's not mixed up in anything dangerous. She can't be."

"Tell me about her. Who does she mix with? Where does she work?"

"I think her and Nicu were an item at one time, but not anymore. As for work," she shrugged, "she was doing some waiting at a club in town. I know she didn't like it, she said it was the pits."

"Do you know which one?" Rachel asked.

"No, she wouldn't tell me."

"Those people who gatecrashed the party, did you know any of them?"

"No, Mum, and please stop with the third degree. I'm not one of your suspects. Ruby comes into the pub near college sometimes, she's a laugh, and everyone gets on with her, that's it. She's no one's bestie, she doesn't say anything much. She drinks and jokes, but when you boil it down, none of us knows much about her."

"Okay, calm down." Rachel didn't want to antagonise Megan. She'd get nowhere if the girl went all moody on her. "This Nicu bloke. Tell me about him."

"Nowt much to tell. Shannon says he's young, good-looking, always has money and gives us the nod when the flat comes free."

"Are you able to contact him?"

Megan was getting annoyed now. "I've already told you. He sends texts, but only to a few people. Then they put the word out."

"This Shannon, is she a new friend of yours?"

Megan nodded.

CHAPTER EIGHTEEN

Day Four

Rachel rang Elwyn first thing the next morning and told him she'd be late. Megan had arranged to meet her friend Shannon in the coffee shop across from uni, and Rachel was going to tag along. She planned to get access to Nicu through Shannon. He needed bringing in. At the very least, she wanted to know why he was looking for Ruby.

"Get Jonny and Amy back on the streets," she told Elwyn. "Ruby hangs out around the hostel area, so tell them to keep an eye on who comes and goes." She cleared her throat. Time to remind Elwyn about later. "Tonight, we've to be at the bar for eight. I'm bringing my stuff with me to work, it's too far to travel back home to get ready."

"Dressy, is it?" he asked.

"Black tie job," Rachel said.

"Once we're done for the day, I'll nip back to my sister's and change. She's not far away, as you know."

Megan was ready and waiting. "We'll have a quick coffee, a word with Shannon, then I'll leave you to it. I've got a lecture later."

"This Shannon. Okay, is she?" Rachel grabbed her overnight bag on their way out.

"She comes from Sheffield and her dad's a GP. Good enough for you?" Megan rolled her eyes. She looked at the overnight bag. "Are you staying out tonight?"

"No, but I'm going to a do, and won't have time to come home and change." Rachel saw the look — puzzled and mildly disapproving. That was rich, given the antics Megan got up to. "I am allowed a social life, you know. Anyway, it's work." This wasn't really a lie — it might well turn out to be. "I'm more interested in who Shannon mixes with. How she got access to this dodgy young man, Nicu, for example." Rachel started the car.

"I've no idea," Megan said, "but please don't go on at her. Shannon isn't *up* to anything. She likes to go out, that's all. Her digs are miles away in Stalybridge. Her dad made her stay with an aunt. Getting back after a night out isn't easy. The trams stop in Ashton and the last one is at eleven, or something stupid like that."

"I don't want you out around the city at night until we've cleared this case up," Rachel said firmly. "It isn't safe and you've come close to this gang as it is."

"Nicu? A gang member? I don't think so, Mum. You don't know a thing, do you? He's a smart lad. He has a job, money, the lot."

"Who does he work for?"

"Some leisure firm."

Rachel was unimpressed. That could mean anything. "Does he talk about the people he works with?"

"I've seen him once, when he let us into the apartment the other night, so I've not spoken to him at all."

"You need to be careful, Megan. This Nicu isn't someone I want you mixing with. Never forget, it was his friends gatecrashed and got you into bother, wasn't it?"

Megan didn't respond, and she remained silent for the rest of the journey. Traffic into Manchester was slow, and it took a good hour before the multi-storey on Oxford Road finally loomed up in front of them.

Rachel parked up, and they crossed the busy road to the coffee shop.

"That's Shannon." Megan pointed to a pretty blonde girl in a window seat, working on her laptop.

Rachel handed Megan a tenner. "You get the coffees."

She went over and sat down opposite the girl, who, intent on her laptop and with earbuds in, took little notice. Smiling at her, Rachel tapped her shoulder.

"Has Megan told you why I'm here?"

The girl removed the buds and nodded. "This has to be all wrong, Mrs King. Nicu is okay. Everyone says so." She frowned. "I won't get into bother or anything for speaking to you? I don't want a gang of morons coming after me."

"Didn't you say this Nicu was okay? So what makes you think that will happen?" Rachel said.

"He is, but he doesn't like people talking, you know, interfering in his business."

"You get the smallest hint that all isn't well, contact me." Rachel passed her card over. Now to get to the real point of the visit. "The next time you get information about an apartment being free, will you contact me?"

Shannon looked doubtful. "I daren't. If I grass and Nicu finds out . . ."

Time to spell it out. "How can it be grassing, Shannon? You insist Nicu isn't a criminal. But you need to know that we're dealing with the murder of one young woman and the disappearance of another — your friend, Ruby. I need to speak to Nicu as soon as possible. He knows Ruby too, and he's looking for her. If he finds her, she may be in real danger."

"I haven't seen her in a while, and if it's that serious, it'll be me in danger for telling you." Shannon shook her head. "I know how these things work. I talk, and one dark night, someone will creep up behind me."

"Help me get these people off the streets, Shannon. Do that and everyone will be safer. Neither Nicu or those he works with will ever know that you spoke to me."

As they were talking, Megan had come over with their coffees.

Shannon looked from Rachel to Megan, and shook her head. "I'll think about it. After the bust the other night, he might lie low for a while."

That was a blow. "Just keep me informed," Rachel said. "Getting these people off the streets is in everyone's interests."

The girl looked puzzled. "I don't understand all the interest in Ruby. She rarely comes to any of the parties."

Rachel chose not to comment. "Will you let me know?"

Shannon nodded.

"How well do you know Nicu?" Rachel asked. "Does he know what course you're on at uni for instance?"

Shannon shook her head. "I'm just another girl in the crowd."

"Good."

Rachel sipped at her coffee. She had what she wanted. With luck, it would lead to bringing Nicu in.

* * *

Back at the station, Rachel found Elwyn at his desk, looking through Agnes's diary.

"The addresses in this are no help. There's new tenants in them now, and no one recalls any pregnant girls having been there before them."

Another dead end. "In that case, we've got nothing," Rachel said.

"Well, we might have something." Elwyn waved the diary at her. "There are dozens of girls' names in here. Just first names against a date, and only some with addresses. I've been trying to work it out, and my best guess is private appointments with Agnes."

"Not official clinic ones?"

"Given that the clinic didn't recognise the names, I doubt it. There are some notes at the back. This name here, a girl called Roxanne, she delivered at the right time and Agnes has starred the entry in red. In the back of the diary there is another red star with an address against it."

"You think that Agnes found her somewhere to live? Where?"

"It's not local. Quite far out in fact. Glossop."

"I wonder why Roxanne felt the need to move so far away?"

"I intend to go and ask her," Elwyn said. "With luck she's still living there."

"I'll join you," Rachel said. She dumped her stuff in her office. "You all sorted for tonight? Suit pressed or whatever?"

"Ah, our date."

Rachel hit him with a folder. "Our *non-date*, moron."

Ignoring the jibe, Elwyn said, "I thought we'd aim to be in Glossop by about two this afternoon. There's no surname, so I can't look her up and tell her we're coming. We'll just have to take pot luck that she'll be in."

"In the meantime, some food and a catch-up with what we've got so far." She paused. "Heard anything from Kenton and his crew?"

"Thankfully, no."

"What does he think? That we're just going to sit on our hands and do nothing? What happened to Akerman is directly linked to our current case, and he knows it. I don't understand Harding either. He just rolled over like an obedient little lapdog."

"Tread carefully, Rachel. Kenton's not a man you make an enemy of. Talk has it that he's a hard boss to work for, and makes a difficult colleague."

"I can do difficult. I can do bloody hard-core if I'm pushed!" She suddenly noticed the empty desks, the absence of chatter. "Amy and Jonny still pounding the streets?"

Elwyn nodded. "Jonny rang in about half an hour ago. They've got nowt so far. Some good news though — Jude rang, says she'd like a word."

Rachel went into her office to ring Jude back.

"We extracted the bullet from Agnes's head, and after scouring that trench, we found the one that I presume killed our unknown," Jude said. "The striations on both bullets are a match. They both came from an old army gun."

"You're telling me that some of those old weapons are still hanging around — and they're usable?"

"Very much so, Rachel. Veterans who didn't hand them back stick them in a drawer, and every so often they surface. They're easily restored to working order if you know the right people. Oh, and good news. We've had the area looked at and there are no more bodies. You can hand the plot back now. I'm sure Mr McAteer will be thrilled."

Rachel decided to keep that information for later. "You know that Salford are investigating the Akerman killing?"

"Yes," Jude said. "We've had our instructions. Hand the scene over to their people — butt out, in other words."

"But you'd started, you'd taken photographs, samples and the like. Er, this is rather delicate, Jude. Refuse if you feel you must, but would you continue to process what you have for us?"

A silence. "Are you ringing me on your own mobile, Rachel? I'd hate to think anyone was listening in, or recording this on the landline."

"Yes, Jude, it's my own personal number."

Rachel heard Jude take a breath. "Okay. I'll do what I can and be in touch. Not a word to anyone, mind, not even your team. If and when I get something, we'll decide what to do with the information. DCI Kenton isn't someone you mess with, Rachel. He doesn't forgive, and he doesn't forget."

Rachel snorted. "I don't give a toss. I just want to find who killed our victims. The Akerman case is ours. I just know it's related to the deaths of Agnes and the unknown."

Tapping on her mobile, Rachel returned to the main office to join Elwyn. "I'm leaving a message for Megan. She has a friend with a link to Nicu. The minute another party is arranged, I want to know."

"If we're to make the do tonight, we should get off. Glossop isn't just down the road, you know."

"A quick coffee and then we'll go."

CHAPTER NINETEEN

Rachel gazed at the countryside rolling past the window. "Why d'you think Roxanne moved all the way out here?" she asked. "It's very pretty and all that, but it's a helluva long way from the backstreets of Manchester where she came from."

Elwyn shrugged. "There's nothing in Agnes's diary to say. But if she was in danger, like our unknown, maybe Agnes wanted to get her out of harm's way."

That made sense. Rachel was beginning to regard Agnes as a caring individual who helped a lot of people, including giving her sister one of her kidneys. "What were they scared of, Elwyn?"

Elwyn smiled. "We'll be sure to ask her."

"I have a theory about Agnes. I don't think she simply helped the girls with advice and their pregnancies. I believe she was trying to get them free of the grooming gang."

"Where did the notion of a grooming gang come from?" he asked.

"DS Colin Howe. He said that the gang Nicu is involved with are into trafficking and grooming young girls."

"If your theory's right, then there's your motive for murder. Agnes was killed to stop her interfering."

"If we're to prove that, we're going to need a lot more evidence," Rachel said.

Roxanne Buckley lived on a council estate. They'd driven through Glossop and were in the countryside on the way out again when it sprawled in front of them.

"I remember this place being built," Elwyn said. "It was meant as an overspill estate to house the people who lived in the condemned terraces of inner Manchester."

"Much trouble?"

He shook his head. "Not that I'm aware of."

They parked up. "Let's see what Roxanne can tell us," Rachel said.

Waiting at the front door, the two detectives could hear children playing inside. A young woman answered, holding a toddler perched on her hip.

She looked at them and grimaced. "You the police?"

"Yes, Roxanne, but you're not in any trouble." Rachel smiled. "We'd simply like to ask you a few questions." Rachel looked around and saw a pair of net curtains across the road give a distinct twitch. "Can we come in?"

"Bloody witch across there never misses a trick," Roxanne said. They followed her into the house. "I'm a registered child minder, hence the kids and the mess. I wasn't expecting visitors."

"You guessed who we were, though."

She looked at Rachel and nodded. "I've been half-expecting you. This is about Jess, isn't it?"

"I don't know, Roxanne, but it might be. What I have to tell you isn't very pleasant, but I have no choice. We are speaking to anyone we can find that was helped out by Agnes Moore."

Roxanne smiled. "She certainly helped me. She's a good woman, but I haven't seen her recently."

"Agnes is dead," Rachel said. "Murdered. But we're here now about another body that was found nearby — that of a young woman. We're trying to identify her. No one has

110

come forward, and no one fitting her description is on our missing persons list."

"But you think it's Jess?" Roxanne asked.

"We've no idea who she is. You are the first person to mention that name."

"I didn't know Jess right well, but we were pregnant at the same time, and that drew us together." She'd gone pale. "I'm sorry. I can't get over the fact that Agnes is dead. It isn't fair."

"When was your baby born?" asked Elwyn.

"Two months ago. I had Nathan and we moved here. Jess still had a week or so to go, and I never saw her again." She looked at the floor. "I don't even know what she had."

"Why did you move out here?" Elwyn asked.

"Agnes sorted it for me," Roxanne said. "The house came free so it had to be quick. I didn't have time to tell anyone."

"You moved here on your own?" Rachel asked.

"Nathan's dad wasn't interested and I've no family. It's a fresh start for me. I like it here, there's plenty of fresh air and no complications."

"And you didn't keep in touch with Jess, or any of the other pregnant girls? You must have seen a lot of each other, attending the same clinic like you did."

"We didn't go to the clinic — Agnes took care of us privately."

"Surely you needed a midwife or doctor when it came to the delivery?" Elwyn asked.

"Agnes was also a midwife. Any major problems and the girls ended up in hospital, although I never knew that to happen. Agnes was great and very capable. She looked after us well."

"That isn't normal practice. Didn't any of you question what Agnes was doing?" asked Rachel.

"Look, we were all in trouble, all running from something. None of us wanted to be found. Attend hospital, go for all that ante-natal stuff and before you know it, your past catches up."

"You were taking a risk, though, so was Agnes," Rachel said.

Roxanne looked at each of them. "How did you know where I was?"

"We found Agnes's diary and took a chance on an address we found written in it. Do you have any idea who would have wanted to harm Agnes?"

Roxanne was very pale now. The reality of what had happened to Agnes must have finally hit her. Placing the toddler in the playpen, she flopped onto the sofa. "I'm sorry. She didn't deserve to end like that. Murder." She shook her head. "Do you have any idea who killed her?"

"No. We're still investigating," Rachel said. "Do you know a girl called Ruby?"

"No. There was no Ruby back then. Mind you, she could be new. Plenty of girls used to go to Agnes."

"What about Nicu?"

"Him?" She sat up, her legs trembling. "He was bad news. Practically kept Jess prisoner. He was the main reason we were all so secretive about being pregnant. That man is an animal. Pregnant or not, he still expected the girls to work just as hard."

"Why not report him to your employers, or the police, even tell a relative what was happening?"

Roxanne shook her head. "We were too scared of what Nicu would do to us if we went to the police. As for family, none of us had anyone we wanted to tell."

Rachel remembered what DS Howe had said about Ruby being on her own, with no one to come looking.

"But Nicu wasn't interested in you, not like with Jess?" Elwyn asked.

"He didn't like me. I don't know why, and I'm glad he didn't. Attracting his attention meant trouble."

"But he liked Jess?" Rachel asked.

"Yes, he was always going on about a special job he had for her, though I've no idea what it was."

Rachel watched her carefully. "You sure?"

"She didn't trust him. Jess was a loner — she did her own thing and wouldn't have thanked me for sticking my nose in. As for the other girls Agnes saw to, I've no idea what happened to them. I'm just grateful she was there, on our side and happy to help the way she did."

Roxanne was nervous all of a sudden. Hearing Nicu's name had done that. "What about Agnes, did you keep in touch with her?" Rachel asked.

"She came round a couple of times at the beginning. Nathan is a sickly baby and she helped. That's what she was like."

"What's your full name, Roxanne?" Elwyn asked.

"My surname is Buckley."

"Do you mind if we check your record at the Medical Centre in Beswick?"

"There won't be any." Roxanne sounded pretty certain of this. "Like I said, the only person I saw all throughout my pregnancy was Agnes. No one else."

Rachel knew that wasn't legal. What was Agnes doing working on her own like that? If she'd been found out she would have been sacked and her nursing registration withdrawn. It was a big risk to take. Had there been an incentive, perhaps?"

"Why no clinic, Roxanne? Agnes was risking everything by treating you on her own. Did she ever ask you for money?"

"No, and I had none anyway."

"So, what did she get out of helping you all?" Elwyn asked. "She took all the risks."

"She was just like that." Roxanne reddened and looked away.

She was lying.

"Did she deliver Nathan?" asked Elwyn.

Roxanne nodded.

"And your friend, Jess, was Agnes looking after her too?"

"Look, Agnes was a friend. She helped us. She didn't do anything wrong!"

"She did, Roxanne. You should have been in the care of the midwifery team at the clinic. I still don't understand why it was necessary for you to be under the radar like that," Rachel said.

"To keep us safe, stop the likes of Nicu finding us."

"Agnes and our unknown victim — we have no idea what they'd done to deserve their fate. We need people to talk to us. You too," Elwyn said.

"Tell us what you know about Nicu," Rachel added. "Did you work for him?"

Roxanne looked away. "He got me a job in a club. A sleazy dive down a back street off Deansgate near the river."

"What sort of job, were you waiting on tables?" Elwyn asked.

She gave a hollow laugh. "Nothing so simple, we had to offer extras. We were sex workers. I hated it, so did most of the other girls. Nicu is trouble, and dangerous."

"We think he might have something to do with those deaths," Elwyn said.

"If the unknown girl is Jess, then I'm sorry but I can't help you." Roxanne folded her arms and sat back.

Clammed up. Talking about Nicu had her scared alright.

"Is there anything you can tell us about Jess that might help us identify the body we found? Did she mention her family, for example?"

"No one who cared. Crap parents who dumped her the minute they could. They split when she was still young. Her father beat her. He broke her arm once, just above the wrist."

"Do you know if she has any other relatives?" Rachel asked.

"Her granny's still alive. Her name's Anita Darwin, and she lives in Levenshulme."

"I still don't understand why you moved all the way out here," Rachel said. "Wouldn't you rather be near people you know?"

"Suits me fine," Roxanne said. "I was lucky, I got help to get out."

"What d'you mean — lucky?" Elwyn asked.

"Out of the city." She stared at them, frowning. "Look, what is this? I've done nowt. You've no right pressing me like this."

"We just want you to be honest with us," Rachel said. "We're looking for a vicious killer, the identity of a victim and a girl on the run. We need all the information we can get."

"Well, I can't help you. I want you to go now. The kids are making a right racket. They need me."

Rachel's instincts told her that the girl was holding back. She was afraid of something — or someone. It was the mention of the name Nicu that'd done it. "What's wrong, Roxanne? What are you afraid of? Speak to us and we will ensure that no one gets to you. We can keep you safe."

Roxanne looked doubtful. She remained silent for a while, obviously considering this. Then she stood up. "Bugger off! Things are okay as they are."

* * *

Rachel and Elwyn headed back towards the Glossop Road. "At one point we were doing fine, then something frightened her," Elwyn said.

"When we mentioned Nicu," Rachel replied. "She's afraid. He could well be the reason she ran. Agnes must have appreciated the danger and got her to a place of safety. It has to be her involvement with the girls that got her killed. We'll speak to Roxanne again. Agnes took a huge risk, and she'd have been the one to pay the price if she was found out. Was it all about protecting those girls, Elwyn, or are we missing something?"

He shrugged. "We don't know enough yet to make that judgement."

Rachel checked her phone and brightened. "I've had a text from Megan's friend Shannon. Nicu is arranging another party this weekend, same apartment and same price. This is our chance to get him, Elwyn."

"All well and good bringing him in, but what evidence do we have?"

"For now, speaking to the bastard will do," Rachel said.

"We can't leave things as they are with Roxanne. She was holding back. We still have questions with no answers."

"Once she knows Nicu has been brought in, things will change," Rachel said. "I'll ask Stella to get an address for Anita Darwin. If our unknown is Jess, we should get a familial DNA match."

They drove down the road towards Stalybridge and the M60, which would take them back to Manchester.

Rachel checked her mobile. "I've got Anita's address. We've got time, we could do this now."

"Okay, whereabouts in Levenshulme?"

"Mathews Lane. Know it?" she asked.

Elwyn nodded. "It's near my sister's."

As they approached the small terraced house, the detectives saw a woman shaking her fist at a group of kids. The second they spotted the car, the lot of them scarpered off down the road.

The woman was small, her face scored with deep lines. Her dyed blonde hair was scraped back off her face, leaving a full fringe that fell over her eyes. A cigarette dangled from her lips.

"Gerrout of it!" she shouted as the detectives got out of the car. "Bloody kids, they should be in school. The parents have no idea. Kids these days need a good battering, teaching who's boss." She registered the detectives' appearance with a frown. "What d'you want? If it's money, you're out of luck."

"Anita Darwin?" Rachel asked.

"Who wants to know?" she asked.

"Are you her or not?" Rachel felt in her pocket for her warrant card. "DCI King and Sergeant Pryce."

"Bloody police! As if I didn't have enough to deal with."

"All we want is a chat. You're not in any trouble," Rachel said. "It's about your granddaughter, Jess."

Anita Darwin looked from one detective to the other, her lined face doubtful. "Can't tell you owt. Me and her never got on. Left here the second she was able, she did."

"We won't take long," Elwyn said.

"You're wasting your time."

Rachel moved forward. "Can we come in just for a minute? We'd still like to ask you some questions about Jess."

Anita Darwin wagged a finger in Rachel's face. "I don't like police, and I don't want 'em in my house. Got that, copper?"

Okay, if that's the way you want it. "Look, this isn't very pleasant, but you give me no choice. We've found a body, and we're trying to exclude the possibility that it's Jess," Rachel said.

If the news bothered Anita, she certainly didn't show it. She dragged deeply on the cigarette and blew out a plume of smoke.

"Would you be willing to give a DNA sample?" Rachel said.

"I warned the silly bitch to mind her step. She were never in, always round them clubs, mixing with God knows who." She stared at Rachel. "You think I'm hard, don't you? Well, stuff you, you lot know nowt!"

"D'you want to tell us about it?" Rachel said.

"Bugger off. I don't have time."

"What about the DNA?" Elwyn said.

She gave a thin smile. "No need, love. It's already on record. Not Little Miss Perfect myself, am I?"

CHAPTER TWENTY

DC Amy Metcalfe looked up and down the busy street. "This is a waste of time," she said. "We've been in all the shops and knocked on so many doors my knuckles have got bruises."

"Ruby's been seen along here, more than once," Jonny said. "We'll get a cuppa and sit in the car for a while. We're parked right opposite the hostel. It's coming up to tea time — you never know, she might pop in for some grub."

"We get all the crap jobs," Amy complained. "It's deliberate, you know. DCI King wants me gone."

Jonny shook his head. "Imagination. She's okay, and this girl does need finding."

"So, where's the cuppa coming from?" Amy asked.

"We'll see if Mavis will sort us out." He smiled.

Amy grinned back. "She likes you."

"She's sussed who my dad is. I reckon she'd do anything for a couple of tickets to City's next match."

"DC Farrell! I think you'll find that's called bribery."

The hostel canteen was filling up. Mavis Smithson was behind the counter serving up pie and chips to the homeless people filing past.

"Got a shift going, if you want it," she called to Jonny. "Tonight. You can go out with one of the blokes and serve up soup around the city centre. You might strike lucky and find your girl."

Amy nudged him. "Sounds like bloody hard work to me. Tramping round Manchester in the dark, feeding folk off their faces on spice. That's no way to spend your evening."

But Jonny wasn't so sure. Mavis was right. It might be a way of finding Ruby.

"The girl with the pink hair, does she turn up regularly?" he asked Mavis, accepting the mug of tea she handed him.

She nodded. "She's been seen. Never in the same place twice, though. But the rough sleepers will know her. Gain their trust and they'll talk to you. We find a couple of smokes usually does the trick."

He smiled at her. "Okay, count me in."

Taking their tea, the two detectives went outside to the car. "We'll have this and then I'll head home. I am doing the night shift, after all," Jonny said.

"More fool you! I'm not mixing with that lot in the dead of night, not even for DCI bloody King."

Jonny looked at her. "She likes initiative, Amy, you know that. If I find Ruby and get her back to the station, it'll be a step up."

"You going for sergeant too? That your plan?" she asked.

"I don't intend to stay a DC for ever. I've got my dad wittering on at me. He was all keen for me to join the family business. I knocked that idea on the head and got nowt but scorn and derision for joining the force. For my own self-respect, I need to show him I'm doing well."

"I thought your dad was a footballer. What's this business?" Amy asked.

"He's retired from the game, not played for a while now. These days he owns a string of sportswear shops all across Greater Manchester. He might be famous and minted, but none of that ever appealed to me."

* * *

Back at the station, Rachel asked Stella to find Anita Darwin's record on the system. Minutes later, there she was. She'd been done for receiving stolen tobacco and booze. Her home was raided and a sizeable haul was found. She'd refused to disclose where the stuff had come from.

Rachel picked up the phone and rang Jude. "Would you do a familial DNA match with our unknown and one Anita Darwin who's on the system. I've been told that Anita might be our unknown's grandmother."

"Not a problem. I'll let you know the minute I get something. About that other little matter, I did as you asked and I've got something. But it's late now and I've left my notes at the lab. I'll catch up with you tomorrow."

That was Jude-speak for she'd got results from the few samples she'd managed to get from the Akerman scene. Rachel was intrigued. What had Jude found?

"It's time to get your glad rags on," Elwyn called to her. "I'm nipping off to change and I'll pick you up here in about an hour."

"Sure you still want to come?" she asked, hoping he didn't feel used.

"Wouldn't miss it. Posh drinks and food in Manchester's latest hotspot — what's not to like?"

She grinned. "What about the people who'll be there? Crooks and charlatans. And then there's Jed." She tapped his arm. "Don't let him put you down. Seeing you with me, he'll try. Just let any jibes float over your head."

"We could ham it up a bit, make him think that you and me . . ."

Rachel's eyes widened in mock alarm. "Absolutely not, DS Pryce. This is work. Remember that, and keep your mind on the job."

As far as Rachel was concerned, it was all just good-natured banter, but there were times when she wondered about Elwyn.

"You working late again, DCI King? Case moving forward?"

Harding. "Yes, sir, we're working on a couple of leads. I'm hopeful we'll have an ID for our unknown before long."

"DCI Kenton asked if you'd found the girl you were chasing after."

That told Rachel she'd been right. The girls, and Ruby in particular, were probably victims of the grooming gang. Why else would Kenton be interested in Ruby's whereabouts? "No, sir, she's a tricky one. Doesn't want to be found."

"When you do find her, let me know. DCI Kenton wants to interview her."

"Do you know what his interest is in the girl?" Rachel asked.

"Not really, but he did mention that she was constantly at that hostel, seeking out Akerman."

Rachel wondered again how much she could trust Harding. What was she thinking? He was her superintendent and had never put a foot wrong. "The cases we are both investigating are linked, sir. Akerman was close to our victim, Agnes Moore. D'you know why Kenton is so interested in Akerman's murder?"

"He has had cases recently with very similar MOs. He is certain it's the same killer."

"We are working on the theory that whoever killed Agnes and the unknown is not the same person as the one who killed Akerman," she said. "Nevertheless, there will be things we should know. Our paths are going to cross at some point, and I didn't find Kenton particularly helpful."

"Any problems, come to me. I'll try and clear the way."

Rachel saw Harding's eyes stray to the pair of heels she was holding.

"Off out?" he asked

"Mr McAteer has invited me and DS Pryce to the opening of a new bar in a tower block he's built in Spinningfields," she said. "I'll give him the good news about the site while I'm there."

He nodded. "It'll do you good to relax."

Rachel couldn't understand why Harding hadn't done any digging on McAteer. Or perhaps he had. If so, and he knew about McAteer's criminal past, why hadn't he said anything?

CHAPTER TWENTY-ONE

Rachel was wearing a midnight blue knee-length dress and black patent high heels. She rarely went anywhere that demanded evening wear and had very little to choose from. Her wardrobe mostly consisted of stuff for work — jeans, shirts, a variety of jackets and comfortable footwear, boots or trainers in the main. The dress she'd dug out for tonight had been bought for a dinner with Alan many moons ago. Fortunately, she was still the same size. She'd only worn the shoes once before and had forgotten how much they pinched her toes.

"My feet will be in ribbons by tomorrow," she complained as they got out of the taxi.

Elwyn grinned. "I thought looking good was everything."

She snorted. "When did I give a toss about how I look?"

"True, you are the exception. You do tend to throw on whatever's to hand."

"Now you're taking the mick, Pryce."

"Smart-looking building." Ignoring her remark, Elwyn cast his eyes skyward. "Right at the top, you say." He looked at Rachel and smiled. "Well, that gives us a problem straight away."

He was talking about having to take the lift. Rachel rarely used them but tonight there was no choice. The restaurant was forty-six floors up.

"I'll grab hold of you and close my eyes," she said. "And not a word to anyone, understand?"

Elwyn laughed. "We can't have the team knowing our hard-faced leader is scared of lifts, can we? It'll cost you though."

"I'll let you into another secret," she said. "I'm nervous. Tonight's escapade is well out of my comfort zone."

He smiled. "Like you said, it's work. Who knows? We might even bump into Nicu. Make the whole evening worthwhile, that would."

"We're certainly going to bump into Jed and that's what's bothering me," she said. "But on the work front, we know Nicu has access to a flat here. From what Megan can remember it was on the twenty-first floor. Mind you, she'll have been well out of it, given the amount of booze she and her mates can shift."

The ride in the lift had Rachel burying her head in Elwyn's shoulder, her eyes closed and her stomach turning over. But the lift moved fast. Only seconds later, he whispered, "We're here."

Rachel smoothed down her dress and ran her fingers through her red hair. "Hard-faced, you said. Right now, I'm feeling anything but."

Elwyn knew how vulnerable Rachel really was, but to the rest of the world she presented a bold front. She was determined not to let it slip. Fighting down her nerves, she gazed around. The bar was packed. There were several faces Rachel recognised, a prominent local MP for one.

"Drinks are over there." Elwyn pointed. "A glass of something will do you good."

"Make it a white wine," she said. "A large one."

"Rachel! Glad you could make it."

Rachel spun round and there he was — Jed — done up to the nines. He had a woman on his arm, blonde, much younger than him and stunning. Rachel stared, she couldn't help it.

"This is Clare," he said simply. Rachel saw Jed's eyes stray to Elwyn, who was just bringing the drinks. "This isn't work," he said. "Or perhaps your sergeant is more than just a colleague?"

Rachel flashed him a warning look.

Jed grinned. "Do you like the place? Cost a bomb, but well worth it. We're fast getting the reputation I want, and the chef I hired for tonight is top notch."

"Shame you've spent all that money," Rachel said, "because your reputation might be tarnished already. One of the apartments here was raided by my Salford colleagues recently. Several people were taken to the station and interviewed."

Jed's face clouded over. "What did the police want? Not drugs, surely?"

"No, trafficked girls," Rachel said with some distaste. "Seems this place is getting a reputation for all the wrong reasons, Jed, despite your best efforts."

"Do you know which apartment it was?"

She had him rattled. "Salford doesn't give much away, but I believe it's on the twenty-first floor. A Romanian individual has access to it." Rachel knew Jed of old, and she watched his face carefully. He knew about it alright.

"I'll look into it. Thanks for the heads-up." Jed turned away.

"Shall we mingle?" Rachel said to Elwyn. "Eyes and ears peeled. That sly bugger knows Nicu. It was written all over his face."

* * *

Jed McAteer went straight to the bar and stood beside a woman waiting to be served. "That lapdog of yours has been causing trouble," he whispered.

The woman smiled at him. "Which particular lapdog is that, darling? As you know, I have quite an entourage these days. Everyone wants to be seen with Leonora Blake."

"Cut the crap, Leo. Tell your people to watch their step. You and Ronan do not want to attract the police's attention. Despite what you think, they're not stupid."

"That's where you're wrong, Jed. The police are precisely that. They follow the trail left for them." The woman nodded towards Rachel. "Your lady friend over there, she's got cop written all over her. Isn't it you who's attracting the police's attention by inviting her?"

"I want to know what they know. You've heard the old adage about keeping your enemies close." He winked at her. "Besides, Rachel's a friend from way back. I'm proud of this building and I wanted her to see it."

"Well, her presence isn't doing you any favours. I mean, look at her. She certainly doesn't do style. You should have taken her shopping first, saved her the embarrassment."

Jed McAteer took Leonora Blake's arm and pulled her, none too gently, into a corner. "Don't badmouth my friends. You've got her all wrong."

Leonora jerked her arm free, stared him in the eye, and slapped his face hard. "Don't you dare put your filthy hands on me again," she hissed. "Or next time it'll be Ronan on your case."

Jed glanced quickly towards Rachel and her sergeant, but they seemed oblivious to this little spat. They were each holding a glass of something, and were looking out of the huge floor to ceiling windows at the city spread out below. He recalled that Rachel didn't do heights. It was probably freaking her out.

He turned to face Leonora Blake. "Be warned, Leo. Your tantrums will come back to haunt you. Ronan's negotiations are at a critical stage. He has too much riding on this to allow a selfish bitch like you to rock the boat. He might be your husband, but he looks after number one. He always has."

"Don't you fucking threaten me! You are nothing but a grimy little hoodlum who's made a bit of cash. You know nothing about Ronan's business, or our relationship. You've got it wrong. Ronan would never allow anything to come between us."

"Get out of my sight, Leo, before I wipe that stupid, self-righteous look off your face."

She swept off to find her husband. No doubt she'd give him an inflated version of events. Ronan would get annoyed, and that wouldn't help anyone. What Jed didn't want was Rachel getting wind of any of this. She was right, both his reputation and that of the building were on the line. If potential buyers heard about the raid, if they even got a whiff of the trafficking allegation, he wouldn't be able to sell another unit.

* * *

"Beautiful, isn't it?" The woman stood behind Rachel and Elwyn. They turned to look at her, and she pointed to Jed. "He has a rare talent, that man. He puts up the most brilliant buildings. This one's done wonders for the area. Property prices have rocketed."

She wore her long dark hair swept off her face and fastened at the back with a diamond comb. She had delicate features and a perfect figure. Rachel reckoned she must be in her late forties.

"Leonora Blake," she said. "My husband, Ronan, and I have the floor below this." She smiled. "I fell in love with the place at first glance. Ronan is so indulgent — he bought the apartment for me at once. It makes a great place to stay when we're in the city on business."

This Leonora woman was doing her best to tone down her northern accent but Rachel wasn't fooled. If she had to make a guess, she'd say she originated from somewhere north of Bolton.

"You're very fortunate," Rachel said.

"Not really. We work damn hard and reap the rewards." Leonora looked back towards the bar. "Have you met my husband Ronan?"

This piqued Rachel's interest. The name had come up in the incident room. Ronan Blake had been down as owning Lion Industries. "No, but I'd like to," she said.

Leonora laughed. "Women are like flies round a honeypot where Ronan is concerned. You're Jed's friends. I saw you with him earlier. How do you know him?"

Straight to the point. Rachel finished her wine. Dutch courage "Oh, our paths have crossed," she said.

"You're police, aren't you? I have an instinct for these things." Leonora smiled. "We're about to do some business with Jed, so I'd love to hear more. We wouldn't want to get involved with him if there was anything about him that wasn't above board."

Charming and as smooth as silk, but she was fishing. "We're currently investigating an incident on some land he owns," Rachel said. "The incident is historical and has nothing to do with Mr McAteer." Well, that was true, wasn't it? Hopefully it was enough to get Leonora Blake off her back.

"I see. He invited you tonight?" Rachel nodded. Leonora smiled. "He's very proud of this place. But make no mistake, he is a businessman. What he's really after isn't praise, it's customers."

Rachel laughed. "Then it's no use looking at us. Not on police wages. But I'm sure the apartments will be snapped up in no time."

"You'd think so, but sales are slow, I believe."

"Leo!" a man called out.

She turned to look. "Ah, Ronan. Come and meet these nice people. They are both police officers."

"Better watch my step." He gave an artificial laugh. "Wouldn't want carting off. Spoil the evening."

"Is there a reason we would do that?" Rachel shot back.

"Not that I'm aware of. Law-abiding citizen, that's me." Ronan smiled but his eyes remained cold.

"You own a number of clubs, I'm told. You were also the landlord of the shops on the site in Beswick that Mr McAteer plans to develop."

"What of it? Anyway, that land is now in Jed's hands."

"We found two bodies on that land. One was dumped there before he bought the site."

Ronan Blake's smile dropped. He regarded the two detectives through narrowed eyes. "Are you accusing me of something? Because, if you are, perhaps I should have my solicitor present." Blake wasn't joking. His tone was serious and his expression was dark, thunderous.

"I shouldn't worry — unless you've got something to hide, of course," Rachel said. "But make no mistake, it is a serious matter. You are down as someone we plan to talk to."

"Well, I can tell you now that I know nothing about any bodies. Have you spoken to McAteer?"

"As I said, it was before his time. Once we have an identity, we'll talk some more. You never know, the young woman might have been a tenant of yours." With a brief smile at the couple, Rachel took Elwyn's arm and walked away towards the window.

"Got him worried, I think," she said. "Fun, isn't it, putting folk's teeth on edge. What d'you reckon to him? He gives me a bad feeling. There's more going on than he shows."

Elwyn merely said, "You need to go easy on the wine."

"Don't you get an instinct about people? I do. Ronan Blake is up to something. He's a bad 'un. My gut tells me so."

He shook his head. "All your gut's telling you is to stop guzzling the wine."

"Don't you feel you could just walk out there?" she said, gazing at the view. "Although huge windows this high up really aren't my thing. Just standing here is making me dizzy."

"Do you want to leave?" Elwyn asked.

"Not yet. I want more of that lovely wine. And didn't Jed say something about a chef? It would be rude not to at least try the food." Rachel grinned.

"What did you say to Ronan?" Jed came up to them, blocking their view. Rachel looked around and saw that the Blakes were about to leave. "Things got too hot for them, I reckon. They certainly don't like the police. That's quite common, you know. We get it a lot."

128

"How much of that wine have you drunk?" Jed asked.

"Not a lot, but then I don't eat much so it goes straight to my head."

"Bloody hell, Rachel," he said. "I wanted to keep that pair sweet. They've got money to invest and I could do with it for my next project."

"Oops! Sorry, love, I might have put my foot in it."

Jed shook his head. "Give it a rest, Rachel."

CHAPTER TWENTY-TWO

"I don't understand you!" Bobby Farrell waved a pair of tickets in his son's face. "The best gig in town, the sportsman dinner, and instead you decide to risk life and limb out on the streets, feeding the homeless." He tossed the tickets onto a table. "And there will be trouble, bound to be, police or not. I don't think you realise how rough it is out there."

Jonny shook his head. "It's work, Dad. I agreed to help because it might get us the break we need. It's called initiative, and finding our missing girl won't do me any harm."

"Attending the dinner is a great opportunity to meet people who can help you in the future. Surely you don't want to stay a copper all your life? I want you in the business with me, so you need to learn the ropes. I want you ready and able to take over when I'm gone." He thrust a portfolio at him. "There it is, everything you need to know about Farrell Sportswear Ltd. I won't go on forever, you know."

Jonny took the folder and flipped through it quickly before something suddenly occurred to him. "You're not ill, are you?"

"One night, Jonny. Meet the suppliers, our main customers. A few drinks, that's all. It's not much to ask."

He hadn't answered the question. Jonny looked at his father. Wasn't he thinner in the face than usual? And pale too. Why hadn't he noticed before? "You are, aren't you, Dad? There's something up."

"No, I'm fine," his father said. "I'm working too hard, that's all. Which is precisely why I need you at my side."

Unconvinced, Jonny decided to take this at face value. "Some other time, Dad, I promise. But not tonight."

"I hope your bunch of no-hopers and that job of yours are worth it, son, that's all I can say."

Jonny was used to his father bellyaching about the job. It was always the same old story. Bobby Farrell wanted his son tied to the business. But it wasn't what Jonny wanted. From as far back as he could remember, he'd set his heart on becoming a detective. He'd let nothing get in the way so far, and this was no time to start. Perhaps if he didn't get the promotion he wanted within the next couple of years, he'd think again.

* * *

"I wondered if you were serious," Mavis Smithson said, smiling. "Here, put this on." She handed him a hi-vis weatherproof coat. "I'll put you with Terry. He's an old hand and knows the ropes, but better than that, he knows the people we deal with and they trust him."

Jonny nodded at the elderly man, who was short and slightly stooped. He held out his hand. "Jonny Farrell." The man gripped it briefly and gave him a half smile.

"You can pull t'trolley, lad, give my arms a rest. By t'time we're finished, we'll have walked a fair way." He pointed towards a sizeable trolley with a long handle. It was laden with all sorts — food, cartons of drink and a selection of plastic bags.

"What've we got?"

"Sandwiches and soup mostly. There's tea and coffee, but we need the hot water for that. Bert does the hot water run once we're set up. Any of them look cold, give 'em one of them bags. They have a hat, gloves and foil blanket. It might be spring but it's chilly on them streets. We have a base just off Piccadilly and another down Deansgate. We'll spend an hour in Piccadilly Gardens and then make our way down Market Street. Better get van sorted. Cop hold of them coats over there. One or two of our regulars could do with sprucing up."

From the base in Beswick, Terry drove the short distance to Oldham Road off Piccadilly. They unloaded and made their way across the tramlines to the gardens.

"'Ere will do." Terry stopped and they parked the trolley against the wall. "Hot water'll be along in a bit. Anyone wants tea, tell 'em to hang on."

It didn't take long before a queue formed and they were dishing out the food and soup.

"Got any fags tonight, Terry?" someone called out.

Terry put his hand in his coat pocket and tossed him a pack. "That's Wolf," he told Jonny. "I know him. He's had some rotten luck, so standing him a couple of smokes does no harm."

Jonny looked over at 'Wolf.' It was clear where he'd got the nickname from. He did look wild, with that long straggly hair hanging around his neck and the full beard.

"He gets about. Knows most of the rough sleepers. Ask him about the lass you're looking for," Terry suggested.

Wolf was leaning against the wall, drinking soup. Jonny went up to him and held out a pack of sandwiches. "Cheese and pickle. They're not bad."

"Not seen you before. What yer after?"

"I'm a volunteer, first night out, so Mavis put me with Terry."

"Bloody do-gooder then." Wolf turned away dismissively.

"Actually, I'm looking for someone," Jonny called after him. "Terry reckons you might know her."

"Who yer after?"

"Our Ruby. You can't miss her, she's got bright pink hair." Jonny watched Wolf's face as he weighed this up.

"What's she to you?" he finally said

"She's family," Jonny lied.

"What's it worth?"

Jonny wasn't sure about giving out money. He knew there was a high level of drug abuse among the homeless. The last thing he wanted was this bloke knocking himself out on spice.

"We've got some coats hanging up over there. You look as if you could do with something warmer, mate."

Wolf didn't look impressed. "A tenner and I'll speak to you."

So much for fobbing him off with a coat. Jonny looked at Terry, who was busy with a group of younger lads. It was taking a risk. Jonny had no way of knowing what Wolf would do with the money, but he needed to find Ruby. Reluctantly, he stuck his hand in his pocket and slipped the money into Wolf's hand.

"By the river off Deansgate, near that new hotel. A club called Leo's. A few weeks ago, she was working there."

"Thanks. I appreciate you telling me." It might be something, then again it might not. Ruby could have moved on since Wolf saw her. But it was all he had. It was still too early for the club scene. Jonny would give it an hour then take off.

"They'll be round to fill us up soon," Terry said. "And then we'll make a move."

"What time d'you finish?" Jonny asked.

"Had enough already then?"

Jonny rubbed his hands together, trying to warm them up. "No, but I've got a lead on that girl, and I want to follow it up. I'll stay here a bit longer and then get off."

"Whatever suits, lad. Appreciated the help. We're always short-handed mid-week."

"D'you get much trouble?" Jonny asked.

"That'll come later. It's always them wandering round the pubs, having their night out. Come closing time, with all that booze inside them, they're less inhibited about what they say. See this lot and fling abuse at them and it gets their hackles up."

Jonny handed Terry his card. "Any bother, ring my station. They'll give you a hand."

"It's okay, lad. The local bobbies keep an eye."

Jonny spent the next hour or so dishing out food and tea. He was amazed at the numbers. They were good natured enough, and grateful for the help. But time was rolling by. It was nearly midnight. Jonny was keen to look at that club Wolf had told him about.

"I'll be off, Terry. Useful night, thanks."

"See you again," he called to Jonny's retreating figure

* * *

Jonny walked all the way down Market Street and turned into Deansgate. The night was busy, with people milling in and out of the bars and eateries. He walked as far as the John Rylands library and then took a right turn past the Magistrates Court. From there he made his way across Hardman Square, through Spinningfields and into New Quay Street. Spinningfields was heaving. Home to Manchester's top restaurants, it was one of his father's favoured stomping grounds.

He knew the hotel Wolf had mentioned. It was about five minutes' walk away. Once there, he'd have to find the club. Time to ensure back-up, should he need it. Jonny was no hero. He'd send a quick text to Amy, telling her where he was going and giving her the rough location of Leo's. After all, he had no idea what he was walking into.

Finding the hotel wasn't a problem. Various old buildings in that area were being refurbished, and the hotel was one of these, sitting amidst an assortment of flats and shops. The club was another matter. He eventually found Leo's tucked around the back of an old factory and off a narrow, dark cobbled alleyway. Easily missed if you didn't know it was here. There were a couple of blokes leaning against the wall outside, smoking, and a burly bouncer at the door.

"Night, mate." Jonny nodded. But the man didn't move. He stood, hands clasped in front of him, blocking the way in.

"What do you want?"

His accent was foreign. Jonny was no expert but he reckoned Eastern European. "A drink. A friend of mine comes here, we're supposed to meet up."

"This friend — he has a name?"

"Adam," Jonny lied. "We were supposed to meet at about eleven. Hope he hasn't got fed up and left." He grinned.

"Move on. There's nothing for you here."

"That's not very friendly," Jonny said. "Don't you want the business? Perhaps I'd better have a word with your boss."

Before Jonny could do or say anything further, he was grabbed from behind and manhandled into the building.

"He's police!" Another Eastern European accent. This one had been rifling through Jonny's pockets and had found his warrant card and mobile.

Jonny's arms were yanked behind him and his wrists tied together with a length of cable. He was then frog-marched along a corridor and thrown unceremoniously into a dark room, where he slid along the wooden floor before crashing against the far wall.

"Stupid copper. Your kind never learn."

"Look, I can explain. This isn't what you think," Jonny said.

"What I think is that you've made a big mistake coming here. And you will pay a high price."

Jonny could just make out the man's shape in the gloom. He was huge, and practically bald. Jonny was trying to fix every detail in his mind when something hard struck the back of his head and he lost consciousness.

CHAPTER TWENTY-THREE

Day Five

Rachel woke the following morning to the shriek of a kettle. She groaned and rubbed her head. What was Megan thinking of, making all that noise?

"Cut out the howling," she yelled, struggling to raise herself onto her elbows.

"Coffee? And take it easy." A hand reached out and helped her to her feet. "You had a skinful last night."

"Elwyn? What the hell are you doing here?"

What had she done? She had definitely not planned on spending the night with Elwyn. What had happened? Rachel racked her brain, but for the life of her, she couldn't remember.

"I live here. This is my sister Ffion's place. You got into a slanging match with one of the waiters. I told them not to give you any more wine and you lost it. I must say, Rachel, you were on cracking form."

"What happened to Jed? Didn't he try to stop me?"

"Oh, you were too much for him. He took off with that woman, Clare. He was happy enough to leave me to deal with you."

Rachel looked down. She was wearing one of Ffion's nighties. "My stuff?"

"On the chair over there."

"Where did I sleep?"

"Not with me," he said hastily. "My sister got you sorted and we left you on the sofa."

"I hope I didn't make too much noise. Are your nieces here? I'd better explain myself."

"They're both away at uni, so you're alright."

"Is Ffion still here?"

"She went off to work a while ago."

"I have to apologise. She must think me a proper headcase."

He grinned. "You're right on that score," he grinned. "But forget it. She's fine."

"I'll get her some flowers or chocolates. What does she prefer?"

"No need. Stop fretting."

Rachel shook herself. It was gone eight and they should both be at work. "Where's my phone?"

Elwyn tossed it to her. "I know I shouldn't have, but I turned the thing off. Mine too. They were pinging half the night. Don't people ever leave you alone?"

"You're right, you shouldn't have. You above all people know the score. I need to be contactable at all times." Rachel checked the missed calls and texts. There were several from the girls — she'd ring them shortly — but there was also one from Amy that had come in a couple of hours ago. Early for her. Must be important. But before she rang her back and got embroiled in the day, Rachel needed a wash and a mug of strong coffee.

Even after a long hot shower, Rachel still felt pretty rocky, so she let Elwyn drive the short distance from Ffion's home to the station. On the way, she phoned Amy.

"Not like our Amy to bother folk so early," Elwyn said. "She tried me too, so she's worried about something."

Amy answered almost at once. "What's so urgent?" Rachel asked.

"Ma'am, I've been going out of my mind," Amy began. "I didn't know what to do."

"Calm down and explain," Rachel said.

"Earlier, when I checked my texts, there was one from Jonny sent late last night. He was on his way to a club in town called Leo's. He'd got a tipoff that Ruby hung out there. Now I can't raise him. His phone is dead and he's not been home. His dad's worried stiff."

"Have you sent anyone to this club to have a look?" Rachel asked.

"A couple of uniforms did that earlier but the building is locked up tight. It's a nightclub, so they open late."

"Can't you get hold of a key-holder?"

"I can't raise anyone to ask," Amy said.

"Do we know who owns the place?"

"A company called Lion Enterprises," said Amy.

That name again. Lion was the company that had previously owned the buildings on the site where Agnes and the unknown had been found, and whose director happened to be Ronan Blake. It was more than mere coincidence. Rachel had suspected that Blake was dodgy from the start.

"Elwyn and I will go and take a look. Have a patrol car meet us there. We might need back-up."

"Jonny is missing," Rachel told Elwyn. "Amy's been trying, but she can't raise him. He took off on his own last night, looking for Ruby at some nightclub."

"There'll be a simple explanation. His battery will be dead. If he was out until the small hours, he's probably sleeping it off. Lucky sod. I could've done with the morning off myself."

"I hope you're right, Elwyn. But I have a feeling he's in trouble. He's gone to a club owned by the Blakes — that pair at the do last night. I didn't like either of them much. How about you?"

"To be honest, I hardly spoke to them."

* * *

When Jonny came to, he found that he was bound to a wooden chair. All he could think of was the photo of Akerman on the incident board, tied to a chair just as he was now. This couldn't just be coincidence.

The giant of a man from the night before was circling his chair, slapping his face periodically. A scar running the length of his left cheek made him look even more menacing in the daylight.

"Ah, it lives." He bent down and thrust his face close to Jonny's. "You are going to tell me what you're doing here. If I am happy with what you say, I may leave you relatively unharmed."

Jonny's head hurt where he'd been hit, and his limbs felt like lead. "I'm a police officer. You are in deep trouble as it is. Don't make it worse for yourself."

The man laughed. "You don't frighten me. You might be the law, but you don't have any power here."

"People will be looking for me," Jonny protested. "You won't get away with this, you know."

This time the laughter was cut short by the sound of a woman's voice.

"Vasile! What the hell is going on? What are you doing?"

Both men looked towards the door. The woman standing there was smartly dressed in a trouser suit. Her dark hair hung loose, reaching as far as her waist.

"Madam!" Stuffing a rag in Jonny's mouth to stop him speaking, Vasile backed away. "This is a troublemaker from last night. I am teaching him a lesson."

"I will not tolerate insubordination," she said. "You do not do this sort of thing without clearing it with me first. Attract the wrong people and we all suffer the consequences."

Jonny had no idea what she was talking about. He squirmed, doing his best to free his hands and rid himself of the rag, until finally he managed to spit the thing out. "I'm a police officer!" he yelled. "So, I'm very much the wrong people! This moron knew that, but he still did this to me."

The woman turned her eyes on the big man, eyes that blazed with fury. "Is this true, Vasile? Is he really police?"

Vasile took Jonny's warrant card from his pocket and tossed it in her direction.

"You bloody fool! Release him at once."

Relief surged through Jonny. He saw the hate and rage in Vasile's eyes. He was furious at having to let him go, and he didn't like taking orders from a woman. Jonny wondered what hold she had over him.

Minutes later, he was free, and his warrant card and mobile returned to him. His head thumped but apart from that, he was no worse for his ordeal. "Is this how you treat your new customers?" he asked the woman. "All I wanted was a drink and to meet up with a friend." He thought it best to stick to his story for now. This was no time to mention Ruby.

"Please accept my apologies. Bring your friend another time, have the night on us. My colleague here can be a little too enthusiastic when it comes to security."

Time to cut and run. "Which way is the exit?"

"Do follow me. I can't apologise enough. You see, we've had a deal of trouble of late, and I have to say, some of the troublemakers were as smartly dressed as you. Vasile takes his role a little too seriously at times. He can be a fool, but being where we are, we need him."

He followed the woman through the bar area. Staff — young girls in the main — were busy cleaning up from the previous night. One or two looked his way. One girl in particular stood out, a blonde, teetering around in high heels. What stopped him in his tracks was the outfit she wore — a bright pink short skirt and matching top. The same as their unknown, and the very clothes Ruby had been wearing when she approached the DCI outside the health centre.

"Why is this place called Leo's?" Jonny asked the woman. "Is that your husband's name?"

"Heavens no. It's mine." She smiled. "My first name is Leonora but my husband always calls me Leo."

* * *

140

Jonny reached the end of the street just as Rachel's car came bombing around the corner.

"He's there!" she shouted, and with a screech of brakes, Elwyn came to a halt.

"Am I glad to see you lot!" Jonny said, sliding onto the rear seat.

Hiding her relief at seeing him, Rachel said, "What d'you think you were doing, Jonny? You do not go off single-handed for any reason. You know that."

"I didn't, not really, I left a text for Amy. But I admit I shouldn't have. I had a pretty grim time of it in there. The place purports to be a club, but it doesn't welcome visitors. Soon as I showed my face, a brute of a security guard tied me up and slung me in a room. I've been there all night. He smacked me across the head as well. If the owner hadn't come along, who knows what would have happened."

Just then, a patrol car roared onto the street.

"Stay put, Elwyn," Rachel ordered. "We're going back to arrest the bloody lot of them."

"No, ma'am!' Jonny said. 'We should wait. Think about it."

"There's nothing to think about. They imprisoned you — you, a detective. We come down on them hard."

"There's girls in there wearing the same outfit as the unknown, the pink number,' Jonny said. 'I think the club is where Ruby worked, perhaps the unknown girl too. I helped the folk from the hostel feed the homeless last night, and one of them knew Ruby. He told me that she was working here a few weeks ago."

"Good initiative, Jonny, but you don't put yourself in danger again, understand?"

"The boss is right. It must have been some ordeal. You look dreadful," Elwyn added.

"I'm not surprised. I reckon I'm lucky to have made it out of there."

Rachel thought about what Jonny had said for a few minutes. He could be right. If they went in mob-handed, they'd get nothing. But on the other hand, the people in there had assaulted and imprisoned a police officer.

"Give me a minute." Rachel got out and went over to the patrol car. "Ring for another car to take one of my officers home," she said. "The rest of you wait here. My sergeant and I are going to have a word with the owner of the club, and they don't like strangers." She smiled. "PC Connor, I've got you on speed dial. Any nonsense and you lot come in quick sticks."

Back in her own car, she questioned Jonny. "Tell me everything you know."

"The place is called Leo's. It's named after the woman who owns it. I didn't get it all, but her first name is Leonora."

Just as she'd thought. This dive belonged to the Blakes. "You're going home, Jonny. Take the day off, recuperate. We'll see you tomorrow."

"A strong cuppa and I'll be fine, ma'am," he said.

"I'm not arguing with you. I'll arrange a lift and then you get on your way." Rachel was already on her mobile. "Stella, I want everything we've got on Ronan Blake and his wife, Leonora. When you have it, text me the info. I also want a warrant to search a place called 'Leo's Club,' and I need it urgently, like right now. Get a PC to pick it up from the court and bring it to me here."

"I should come with you," Jonny said.

"You'll do as you're told. You've taken a knock to the head and you need to rest up."

CHAPTER TWENTY-FOUR

"Police!" Rachel shouted, and banged her fist on the locked club doors. "Open up."

"Someone's coming," Elwyn said. "How do we play this? You do remember that last night we were drinking with this woman?"

"Makes no difference, she's dodgy. I sensed it when I was talking to her and after what happened to Jonny, it seems I was spot on."

A man answered the door. Tall and wearing a suit, he was definitely not the brute Jonny had described.

"We want to talk to Leonora Blake." Rachel flashed her warrant card at him.

"She's not here," he said, beginning to shut the door.

"Oh yes she is," Rachel said. She had spotted the fancy car parked a few metres further up the road. A car like that round here could only belong to the Blakes. "Get her now or suffer the consequences."

"Darling! I didn't realise." Rachel recognised Leonora's voice. "You're Jed's friend. Do come in." Leonora came to the door, a wide smile painted across her face. "Can I do something for you?"

"For starters, you can tell me why you thought it necessary to assault and imprison one of my officers."

"That was a mistake," Leonora said.

"You've got that right," Rachel said. "I could have the lot of you arrested."

"The employee concerned has issues. His command of English isn't good. He misunderstands things, and takes his duties far too seriously. It won't happen again," Leonora said.

"Go and find him," Rachel said.

"I really don't think that's a good idea. Vasile has a quick temper. He forgets himself."

Rachel folded her arms. "We aren't leaving until we've spoken to him."

Leonora Blake turned and nodded at a young woman sweeping the floor nearby. She too was wearing the pink outfit.

"Do you employ a lot of girls like her?" Rachel asked.

"They're students mostly. They need the money and can stand the late nights."

"Do you know a young man called Nicu?" asked Rachel.

Leonora laughed. "I know a lot of young men, but the name isn't familiar."

"What about a young girl called Ruby? Jess Darwin? Ever employed either of them?"

Leonora Blake looked at each of the detectives in turn. "What is this? What do you imagine I have done?"

"Apart from what you did to my officer, we're investigating murder, Mrs Blake. It appears that the people you employ here are not averse to using violence with little or no provocation. Plus, one of the victims was wearing your work uniform."

"I'm sure you're wrong. Those little pink outfits can be bought anywhere on the High Street. It's a coincidence, that's all."

"Okay. Your employment records," Rachel demanded.

Leonora Blake looked surprised. "I'm sorry, but you can't do this. We have rights. You can't barge in here and demand to see anything you choose."

Rachel moved a little closer to the woman. "Have it your way. But be warned, I'll have a warrant in my hand within the hour, and then my people will tear this place apart." She gave Leonora a moment or two to consider this. "Sure we won't find anything? No contraband or drugs, for example?"

"What sort of place do you think we run here?" Leonora asked indignantly.

"That's what I intend to find out."

"Wait here. I must let my husband know what has happened," Leonora said.

"Where is your husband?" Rachel asked.

"Out on business. This place belongs to me. I'm perfectly capable of running it without him under my feet."

"Watch her, Elwyn," Rachel ordered. "We don't want them clearing the place before the search."

Rachel peered in through the door. She saw a large bar area with a number of tables. Tucked in a far corner, she spotted a young girl who appeared to be trying to keep out of sight.

"Are you alright?" Rachel went inside and approached her. "We're not here to do you any harm. You're quite safe."

The girl who emerged from the shadows was painfully thin. She was dressed in the familiar pink uniform.

"My English is not good," she said.

"Where are you from?"

"Romania." She glanced furtively around the room, her dark eyes fearful. "Mrs Blake will not like me talking to you."

Rachel smiled at them. "Mrs Blake is in trouble, so don't worry about her."

The girl backed away. "I must go. I have work to do."

"How did you find this job?" Rachel asked.

"Vasile arranged everything. He said there was work in the UK and brought me to this club."

"Do you know his full name?"

"Vasile Danulescu."

"What's your name?" Rachel asked.

"Back to your duties!" Before the girl could reply, Leonora Blake came and stood between them. "Take no notice of her, Detective. Her English is patchy, apart from which she's a liar."

"She looks half-starved to me. How hard are you working these girls, Mrs Blake? Or perhaps she's an addict. Is that it?"

"I have no idea. What my staff do in their own time is their affair," Leonora said.

"Keeping your girls hooked on drugs is one way of maintaining control. Is that the case here?"

Her face twisted in anger, Leonora Blake stalked towards Rachel. "You know nothing about this business. We offer a good night out. The punters like the girls, they are happy to spend money, buy them drinks. Everyone wins. Alright? I want you to go now."

"You win, you mean," Rachel said. "I doubt the girls get much out of the deal. I'm waiting for the warrant, and then my people will go through this place until they find what I need."

"I will not allow that to happen."

Rachel spun round and saw a man standing at the entrance, arms folded, filling the doorway. This had to be the one who'd terrified Jonny.

"I take it you're Vasile, the brute who assaulted my officer." As she spoke, Rachel pressed the alert for PC Connor. It was time to wrap this up. They needed to get this pair down to the station for questioning before things got nasty.

Vasile walked closer. "You know my name, I see. Well, you would do well to forget it and leave now. That way no harm will come to you."

Elwyn was at her side immediately. "Threatening an officer is a serious offence," he warned.

"You do not scare me," Vasile said.

PC Connor and four officers stormed into the club. Rachel breathed a quiet sigh of relief. "Arrest him," she said to Elwyn. "And her. Make sure she's cuffed."

"The warrant isn't ready yet," PC Connor whispered.

"It's okay. Round up everyone in the building and bring them in here, particularly the girls. I want to know where each one came from, and if any of them are being kept here against their will."

"My husband will have your job for this," Leonora fumed.

"You can contact him from the station. And I suggest you think about a solicitor while you're at it."

Rachel watched the officers escort Vasile and Leonora out of the building. "Phew! He's some size, isn't he? I wouldn't want to meet him on a dark night."

"I'd like to know why a small backstreet club needs muscle like him," Elwyn said.

"I think he's more than just muscle, Elwyn. I doubt those girls are here by choice. Vasile keeps order, arranges their transportation from wherever they come from. I spoke to a girl just now — young, pretty and probably an addict. Being kept here against her will, I reckon. Put a call out for Ronan Blake. Let's bring him in and see what he has to tell us."

* * *

Rachel left the officers searching the club and went back to the station, keen to get on with the interviews. "Stella, do you have anything on the Blakes yet?"

"Ronan Blake is a businessman, done well for himself. He has no record and neither does his wife."

"Would you check that those are their real names? Go back a while, to before his businessman days. What about Vasile Danulescu?"

"That one has a record as long as your arm. The trouble is, not a single charge has ever stuck. Each time he's arrested, he gets out on a technicality."

Rachel was determined that this time would be different. Danulescu was probably guilty of people trafficking, with Leonora complicit in the offense.

"Has he been processed?" she asked.

DC Amy Metcalfe nodded. "He was wearing a ring, ma'am, a huge gold thing with a diamond in the centre. I'm thinking about the mark on Agnes Moore's face. If he killed her, it might still have her DNA on it."

"Good call, Amy. Contact Jude, get her to do the tests." Rachel turned to Elwyn. "We'll interview him first."

"I doubt it'll be pleasant. We'd better take a couple of uniforms for protection. He's easily riled and I bet he packs some punch."

"Let him try!"

Rachel nodded at two of their uniformed colleagues who were sitting at their desks. "You pair will join us. Wits about you, mind. This one fancies himself as a tough guy." Grabbing the files on the murders of Agnes, the unknown and what little they had on Akerman, she beckoned to Elwyn.

"I want to talk to each of the girls working at that club in turn," she told Amy on their way out. "Keep them sweet, but don't allow them to leave. We need to know where they came from and the circumstances of their employment at that club."

"There are only four of them. One is British and the others are foreign," Amy said. "If any of the foreign girls are here illegally, immigration will have to be told."

"For now, I'm more interested in their welfare. Where are they?"

"In the soft interview room," Amy said.

"Stella, get onto social services and give them the heads-up. Once I've spoken to them, they'll need finding safe accommodation," Rachel said.

The two detectives and the PCs entered the interview room. The uniforms stood at the back by the door, while Rachel and Elwyn sat opposite Vasile Danulescu and his solicitor.

Rachel made the introductions and got straight to business. "Tell me about the club. What sort of a place is Leo's?"

Vasile stared at Rachel, his face impassive. "It's a dive. People go there to drink, to ogle the girls. It's not complicated."

"What is your role?"

"I do not have one," Vasile said simply.

"What were you doing there last night?" Rachel asked.

"I was merely a customer. Later on, Mrs Blake asked me to control an aggressive customer." He shrugged. "I'm happy to help."

"Leo's has security staff, why couldn't they sort it out?"

"I do not know. There was a problem, I sorted it. Mrs Blake was grateful."

"Tell me about the girls. Where do they come from?" Elwyn asked.

"I do not know. Mrs Blake hires them."

"At least one I spoke to is Romanian, like yourself. Surely you must have spoken to her?" Rachel said.

"You're not really interested in the girls, are you?" Vasile said. "You are after something else. What do you really want?"

"That's where you're wrong, Mr Danulescu. I'm very interested in those girls, particularly when they end up dead or missing."

He shrugged. "I do not know what you're talking about."

"We're investigating the murder of a young woman. She was found wearing the same clothing as the girls who work in the club. Surely you must have noticed that she was missing?" Rachel said.

"I've noticed nothing. They all look the same to me. I go there to drink and I mind my own business."

He was a cool customer alright, composed, well-mannered and so far, he hadn't put a foot wrong.

"Currently you have one missing girl, and she's giving you the run-around. Her name is Ruby." Rachel watched him closely for his reaction.

"I do not know her."

When he heard the name, Rachel thought she detected a small change in his demeanour. His eyes narrowed and his hands clenched. He knew the girl alright. All her instincts told her that this man was a killer, but she needed solid evidence.

149

"I believe you are involved in trafficking girls and enslaving them. You ensure they're pliant by getting them hooked on dope."

"Rubbish! You are deluded. The girls go to Mrs Blake looking for work. She is doing them a favour taking them on."

"Do you know a young man who goes by the name of Nicu?" she asked.

"No."

"He isn't someone you task with finding the girls when they go missing, or sourcing new candidates?"

"I do not know him. You are wasting both your time and mine questioning me like this. You have no evidence that I have done anything unlawful."

This smug reply irritated the hell out of Rachel. "You assaulted one of my officers and held him all night against his will. For now, that is all I need."

"That was a mistake," he conceded. "The way he acted, I mistakenly thought he was a troublemaker. I put him somewhere safe, intending to phone the police. However, the club was busy, Mrs Blake needed me and I forgot." He paused for a moment. "Please give your colleague my heartfelt apologies."

Rachel had heard enough. She needed more evidence. Her gut said this man was as guilty as hell, but that would cut no ice with the CPS.

CHAPTER TWENTY-FIVE

Rachel and Elwyn were on their way back to the incident room. "He is part of the trafficking ring, I'd stake my career on it," she said. "He's been interviewed before. He knows the ropes. Nothing we said bothered him in the slightest."

"He's certainly been arrested before, but like Stella said, nothing stuck." Elwyn shook his head.

Harding and Kenton were waiting for them in the incident room.

"My office, DCI King," Harding ordered.

Rachel followed him and Kenton. She'd no idea what this was about.

"You've brought Danulescu in," Kenton said. "Why?"

The look on his face said it all. The Salford DCI was furious. But why? "He imprisoned and assaulted one of my officers," she retorted. "Apart from which, I believe he's part of a trafficking ring. We've got four girls waiting to be interviewed. Three of them are foreign, and one has already told me that it was Danulescu who brought her into the country."

"I'm afraid he will be coming with me, and my people will speak to the girls."

Rachel was determined that he wasn't getting away with this. But how to stop him, particularly when Harding did nothing to back her up? "Oh no you don't! Danulescu will remain in custody here. I haven't finished my investigations yet. There may be evidence among his belongings to show that he killed one of our female victims. I'm having a ring of his processed as we speak."

"Look, I'm sorry, I don't like doing this, but arguing the point won't get you anywhere. The trafficking case is mine, and Danulescu is coming to Salford to be interviewed."

"Sir?" Rachel turned to Harding.

"It's out of my hands, Rachel. DCI Kenton has the full backing of the ACC in this instance."

Bloody bureaucracy! "Have you met Danulescu? Do you know who you're dealing with?"

Kenton nodded. "I've interviewed him on several occasions."

"But have you got enough evidence to charge him? Are you sure the girls will speak up against him in court? The four I have here are terrified. I doubt they'll say anything useful at all." Kenton seemed to hesitate — he wasn't sure how to answer that one. "You haven't got anything, have you? So why take him?" She looked from one man to the other, and then it hit her. "Please tell me you're not offering this man a deal! Surely, he's not going to walk away from this?" Neither said a word in response. "Because evidence or not, you know as well as I do that he's as guilty as sin."

"What happens to the man is no longer your concern," Kenton said at last.

Not good enough. "That's where you're wrong. I'm trying to build a case against Danulescu. I think he hit one of our victims before he killed her. His ring could hold the proof I need. If I'm right, it puts him at the scene of her murder." Rachel looked at Harding for help. "Are you going to allow this, sir?"

"I have no choice. Perhaps DCI Kenton will allow you speak to Danulescu once his people have processed him."

Rachel looked at Kenton. "Well?"

"It's a possibility," he said. "We'll keep in touch."

Rachel was seething. "Are you taking him now?"

Kenton nodded. "I have a car outside."

"Does Danulescu know?" she asked.

"His solicitor has been told, so yes, he does."

Rachel shook her head. "He's had this get-out clause planned all along. That man is playing you. How much d'you bet he gives you nothing useful?"

Rachel could see Kenton growing more annoyed with every word she said. "He's our way into a trafficking ring we've been trying to crack for months. He will give us names, routes, but more important the name of the local head man. Danulescu is small fry. It's the boss I'm really after, DCI King."

"You're confident that he'll talk?" she asked.

"We have been building a case against him for a while," Kenton said. "It's accept the offer or go to prison for a long time. Danulescu realises it's the end of the road for him, so he has no choice."

"Can I suggest that you leave the girls with us? I and a female DC will speak to them. They are very frightened but we may get something."

Kenton nodded. "Okay, but I want a full report, and my officers will have to speak to them at some point."

Rachel nodded. "It's my intention to find them temporary accommodation. I'll inform immigration, and social services will help with housing them."

Kenton didn't put up an argument. It was obviously Danulescu he wanted — he didn't seem particularly bothered about the girls.

Rachel looked at him. "This head man you're after, you must have a theory."

"I do, DCI King, but it isn't up for discussion."

Kenton had won. Rachel was deflated but still furious as hell. He'd breezed in, laid down the law and snatched her arrest from under their noses — all with Harding's blessing.

"You can't fight it, Rachel," Elwyn said when she told him what had happened.

"This head man they're after must be some catch for them to offer a deal."

"Any idea who he is?" Elwyn asked.

"Kenton wouldn't say, but we've got all the pieces to the puzzle now. We should be able to work it out. But I'm not finished with Kenton yet. Danulescu knew Akerman, and he in turn knew Agnes. There's a link, and I need the opportunity to explore it. I want a firm appointment to speak to Danulescu before he walks."

"What can you do?" Elwyn asked.

"Give me minute. I won't be long."

Eager to collar Kenton before he drove away, Rachel flew out of the incident room and down the stairs, spotting his car at the main entrance. Danulescu was just being escorted to a seat in the back. "Kenton! A word."

He stood beside the car door, just about to get in. "It's all been said, Rachel."

"Maybe, but I'm not happy with the way things have been left. I want to be party to the interviews. I have questions—"

She got no further. At that moment, a single shot rang out. The bullet struck Danulescu and he dropped like a stone. Kenton pushed Rachel to the ground, covering her with his body.

* * *

Danulescu was dead. A single bullet had entered his right temple and exited the opposite side, embedding itself in the station wall, just centimetres from where Rachel had been standing.

She wasn't even sure what had just happened. Kenton gently helped her to her feet, slowly back to the incident room and sat her down. "Tea," he said to Amy.

Elwyn hurried up to them. "What happened? I heard the noise."

"Someone shot at us," Rachel said, staring into space.

"Not us — Danulescu," Kenton corrected. "Whoever he was working for was making sure he wouldn't talk."

"It's broad daylight! A police station! Who are these people?" Elwyn said.

"Not people you mess with, believe me." Kenton was kneeling in front of Rachel. "You're okay. Shame you came out when you did. What did you want?"

His voice was gentle, reassuring, not at all that of the man she'd been arguing with in Harding's office. "I . . . wanted to arrange an interview. Danulescu knew things. He could have helped with the murders we're investigating."

"Someone should take you home," Kenton said. "I think you've had enough for one day."

"Who are these people? Who would shoot their own before allowing them to speak to the police?" She looked at Kenton. "You spoke of a head man. Who is he?"

"Even if I knew that, I couldn't tell you. All I can say is that he's in Manchester, with links to organised crime. Danulescu's evidence would have nailed him."

"Look at me, I'm shaking." Rachel held out her hand. "You must think I'm a right soft cow."

"Certainly not. I know your reputation, Rachel. You're a first-class detective."

Praise now. So why all the secrecy? Why keep everything so tight? He must realise that she could be trusted to keep the information to herself. Or perhaps he thought she couldn't. Her head was swimming. Danulescu, Nicu, Ruby, the names spun around in her brain but she couldn't quite catch hold of them. This man at the top linked them all, but who was he? Kenton wouldn't share his theories, so she'd have to work it out for herself. Their investigations overlapped, so had he come within their sights already?

She took the tea Amy offered her and sipped the hot, sweet liquid. Curiosity was eating at her. Organised crime was active on her patch. This was nothing new, but people trafficking was. Up until now it had mostly concerned drugs, armed robbery and money laundering. Kenton and

Harding knew more than they were saying, and Rachel was determined not to be kept out of the loop. It just wasn't an option. In her mind, she listed the individuals involved with the murders. Danulescu had worked for Ronan Blake. She didn't know a great deal about Blake. He had no record — perhaps that was deliberate. His wife was currently being held. As far as Rachel was aware, her husband had made no attempt to contact her or provide a solicitor. Why?

"Have we brought Ronan Blake in yet?" she asked Elwyn.

"We can't find him," Elwyn said. "His mobile is switched off and he's not at home. It looks suspiciously like he's done a runner."

"Blake is no concern of yours, Rachel," Kenton said. "Leave him to me."

CHAPTER TWENTY-SIX

Ten minutes later, Rachel was still shaking, and she had the most awful ringing in her ears. "I'll be alright," she said in response to Elwyn's concerned looks, "as soon as I get my head round what just happened."

"A man was shot dead only inches away from you," Kenton said bluntly. "You need to go home."

"There's the girls from the club, and Leonora Blake. They all need to be interviewed."

Kenton frowned. "I'll leave the girls to you, but I want to interview Blake."

His expression gave nothing away. Rachel couldn't tell if Kenton wanted to speak to Leonora because she was Danulescu's employer, or for some other reason.

"Are the Blakes part of this?" she asked him. "It's interesting that Ronan Blake is now missing."

He said nothing in reply, sticking his hands in his trouser pockets and going over to the windows. He checked his mobile. "Armed response was on the ball. They've done a sweep of the area but found no one. It looks like whoever shot Danulescu got clean away."

"Blake isn't his real name, is it? We've checked him out and can't find anything on him further back than twenty years. So, who is he?"

"You're very astute, Rachel, but I can't discuss this with you. For now let's just say that the Blakes are persons of interest."

"Of interest to us both, in that case."

"Your car is waiting outside," Kenton said. "Leave the rest until you feel better."

"We'll interview the girls tomorrow," Rachel told Elwyn and Amy. "Get them sorted for tonight."

* * *

Given the choice, Rachel would have remained at work. But Kenton was adamant. He wanted her gone. He was probably right. She must be in shock. But the case was bugging her. On the journey home she closed her eyes, leaned back and went over what they had. How was Agnes's murder linked to that of Danulescu and the trafficking gang? The answer was simple enough — because of the girls. The evidence for that was the outfit Ruby was wearing that day outside the health centre. Their unknown had been found in the same one, which meant that Ruby probably worked at Leo's too. Then there was the pink hair found on Agnes's sofa, suggesting that she had been sheltering the girl. Akerman was in a relationship with Agnes, and they had the hostel in common. Rachel presumed that Agnes's involvement was down to visiting the hostel and becoming concerned about what she saw there, and what she was told. She must have been trying to get them away from whatever they were involved in.

No matter which way Rachel looked at this web of connections, it all came back to the Blakes. They owned the club and provided the pink outfits the girls wore to work in. Despite what he said at interview, Rachel was convinced that Danulescu was employed by the Blakes as muscle. Poor Jonny would testify to that. It was too much of a coincidence for Rachel. Ronan Blake had to be the prime suspect for head man of the trafficking gang Kenton was chasing.

Taking her mobile from her pocket, she rang Amy at the station. "Remind me, what did we find on the Blakes?"

"Aren't you supposed to be resting, ma'am? The case will wait."

"Just tell me what you've found."

"Very little," Amy said. "Ronan Blake has built up his business over the last twenty years. He's invested in shops, cafes, clubs and property. During that time, he's never been in trouble, and none of his clubs have ever been busted, until we stormed in."

"You're sure? No drug dealing? Nothing?"

"Not as far as we can see, ma'am."

"Dig a bit deeper, Amy. Find out where the money came from to buy those businesses. The Blakes aren't as law abiding as they appear. I want detail and quick. I suspect Ronan Blake changed his name at some point, probably before he adopted the respectable businessman persona."

"I'll do my best, ma'am."

"Get Elwyn to help you. Has Kenton gone?" Rachel asked.

"He left soon after you did. He's had Leonora Blake transferred to Salford."

"That speaks volumes. He obviously suspects her, and her husband too."

* * *

Arriving home, Rachel saw Belinda Bellamy's car on Alan's drive. She couldn't help smiling to herself. They made an odd couple, but as long as Alan was happy, that's all that mattered.

Her eldest girl was surprised to see her. "God! Has the world ended? What are you doing home?" Megan exclaimed. "Or perhaps you've forgotten something?"

The last thing Rachel wanted right now was a spat with Megan. "Oh, I was shot at," she said nonchalantly. "Downside of the job." She put her keys and mobile on the hall table and went into the sitting room. She poured herself a stiff drink.

"You're joking?" A shocked Megan followed her. "You're not, are you? Your hand's shaking. Are you okay, Mum?"

"I'm not hurt if that's what you mean. But I am pretty shaken up, and I've got a horrible noise in my ears." She took a swig of the brandy. "A man was killed within inches of me. It only took an instant. He dropped like a stone."

"Will it be on the news?" Megan asked.

"Probably."

Megan threw her arms around her mother. "Has it got something to do with the other night? I know I go on and say stuff, but I don't mean it."

"This isn't your fault, Meggy. The job can be dangerous, we shouldn't lose sight of that. As for the other night, it is loosely connected. I reckon your mate Nicu is mixed up with some dodgy people."

"Well, he's not my mate. Me and the others have been talking, and we've decided not to risk going again."

That was something at least. "The latest contact with Shannon about the party — do nothing, we'll take over from here. If Nicu turns up, we'll have him."

Megan nodded. "You will be careful, won't you? I know the job's important and all that, but me and Mia need you."

Rachel nodded. "I know that, love. Today was a one off. That sort of thing doesn't happen very often." She downed the rest of the brandy.

"Why don't you have a lie down? I'll get some tea together and give you a shout in a while."

Rachel nodded. A rest would do her good — if she could sleep, that was. Given how her mind was racing, Rachel feared she might never sleep again.

* * *

It was dark. The alleyway was shrouded in shadow, and Ruby was becoming more afraid by the minute. Anything could happen and no one would know. The back alleys of Manchester were dangerous at night, everyone said as much. It would have been safer to stay by the shops on Market Street, but that was out of the question. Ruby daren't risk being found. She pulled the old blanket around her bony shoulders and huddled deeper into the doorway. She was cold. She'd been coughing all day and her chest hurt. She felt dreadful.

"Want a swig, love?" he said in a deep gravelly voice, holding a whisky bottle just out of reach.

"Don't drink."

"Liar! I've seen you in the gardens off your face. Go on, take a good long swallow. Warm you up."

This was too much for Ruby to deal with. She'd been on the run all day and was exhausted. All she wanted was to close her eyes for an hour and doze in peace.

"Got any dosh?"

"No," she said.

"Girl like you, pretty an all, you should be pulling in a small fortune. Do yourself a favour, get your backside down Deansgate. Them clubs are turning out about now."

"Leave me alone. I need to sleep."

"You're missing out on a fortune. Don't care what they spend, them rich types."

"Leave me be. I'm not going anywhere."

"I know you. You're the one dodging them Romanians. Scared witless aren'cha?" He laughed.

"Not me."

"Sorry, love, but if you go about with hair like that, folk will remember you. A bloke were asking about you just tonight. Reckons there's a drink in it for information."

"Look, it's not me, okay? Leave me to get some rest. Maybe then we can go down Deansgate and see what pickings there are."

"Fancy a smoke?" He held out a roll-up. "You must be cold. Why not come back to the gardens with me? One of the blokes has lit a fire. We'll have a drink and get warmed through."

Ruby pulled hard on the cigarette. The smoke filled her lungs, bringing on another coughing fit. It made her feel strange and woozy. She threw it on the ground. "This is cut with spice! Do one!" She turned to go. "I'm off, and don't follow me."

She'd had enough. She was too ill to live like this, and Nicu was getting closer. Sooner or later someone would dob her in and she'd be dead. Agnes should have been her salvation, but she was gone, and there was no one else. Or was there? The hostel! Mavis might help her. She appeared hard on the surface, but the woman wouldn't do what she did if she wasn't a good 'un at heart.

CHAPTER TWENTY-SEVEN

Day Six

Rachel woke early the next morning with a thumping headache. Miraculously, she had slept. She put on her dressing gown and went downstairs.

Alan was in the kitchen. He smiled. "I'm fixing breakfast for this pair. Want some?"

"Coffee will do."

"Meggy told me about your ordeal. How d'you feel?"

"I'll be fine," she said. "I don't like fuss, as you know. I'm best left to process this on my own."

"Look, Rachel, we want to help. You could have been killed, for heaven's sake. That sort of experience leaves its mark. You should take some time off."

Rachel shook her head. "I'm a tough cookie, don't forget. Work'll sort me, not sitting around doing nowt."

The house phone rang. Mia answered it. Handing the receiver to her mother, she pulled a face. "It's Superintendent Harding."

"Sir?"

"I want you to take some time off, Rachel. You had a narrow escape yesterday. You'll need a while to get your head together."

Alan was bad enough, but the last thing Rachel wanted was Harding getting all fussy. "I need to work, sir. My team are in the middle of a murder case. Now is not a good time to go off sick. I mean, I wasn't actually shot. There's nothing wrong with me."

"How about counselling then? Talking the experience over might help."

"I'll think about it. For now, sir, I'd appreciate being allowed to get on with the job."

"Okay. Well, come and see me when you get to the station. There are a couple of things we need to discuss."

That sounded ominous. What, wondered Rachel, did he have in mind?

"You're not going in?" Alan said, shaking his head. "I wish you wouldn't. Meggy's at home today, she can look after you."

"Meggy has studying to do. And what would I do hanging around the house all day? I'd just fret about the case and get on her nerves."

Rachel grabbed her coffee. They meant well, but just listening to them was stressful. It made her feel as if her head was about to explode. She needed to get to work. The case would keep her busy and, with luck, help her push yesterday's incident to the back of her mind.

"You've no car. Want me to give you a lift?" Alan offered.

"I'll take the train. It's not a problem. It only takes twenty minutes, and Elwyn can pick me up at Piccadilly."

"There's no helping some people." Alan walked off to check on the girls. "I'll do tea for them then," he called back.

* * *

Elwyn opened the car door and squinted up at her. "Here's something to cheer you up. We've had a break. Late last night, Ruby turned up at the hostel asking for help. The place was full, and at first Mavis Smithson was all for sending her packing but then she realised the girl was seriously ill. She sent for an ambulance and Ruby was taken to the MRI. She's got pneumonia. She's in a bad way."

Rachel smiled. "Pink hair Ruby? Have we put a guard on her room?"

"Yes. Oh, and Kenton's been sniffing around. The minute she's able, he wants to speak to her."

"Any chance we can get to her first? I don't want that man scaring her off, Elwyn. Ruby has a foot in both camps. She knew Agnes and she worked in that club, Leo's. She knows things, I'd stake my job on it."

"And Harding's on the prowl," Elwyn said. "He told us that you're coming in, and to go easy."

"Yes, I know, he rang me at home. He also wants me to take time off, have counselling and heaven knows what else." She rolled her eyes.

"But you're not keen?"

"Absolutely not. I'll get over what happened in my own way." She changed the subject quickly. "Will the hospital let us know when Ruby is up to talking?"

"Yes, the PC watching her is one of ours," Elwyn said.

Rachel nodded. "We should speak to those girls we brought in. Did you find them all a bed for the night?"

"Yes. They should be at the station about now. I've arranged an interpreter. At least one of them doesn't have good English."

As soon as they arrived at the station, Rachel went straight to her office. She was about to get stuck into her voicemail messages and emails when a PC knocked on her door.

"There's a couple downstairs asking to see a detective, ma'am. They reckon they're the victims of a scam."

"Did they say what sort of scam?"

"No. They just said it was a bit delicate."

Rachel didn't have time for this. It'd be a couple of suspicious phone calls or a dodgy email. "DC Farrell is in the main office. Ask him to speak to them."

Now it was Harding's turn to interrupt her. "Can I have a word?" Without waiting for a reply, he came into her office and sat down.

"Certainly, sir."

"DCI Kenton is insisting you stay out of his investigation," he began. "You expressed an interest in being party to the impending interview with the Blakes. He has refused."

"Can he do that?" she asked.

"He is investigating a high-profile case, and he also has the ear of the ACC."

How dare they discuss this behind her back! "Has he brought Ronan Blake in yet?"

"No," Harding said.

"The man has gone to ground. Ronan Blake is at the centre of this. I believe he's the man Kenton is after."

"You could be right," Harding said. "I've had a look at the case notes for the murders you're currently working on. Put that with what Kenton is investigating and Blake certainly looks the part."

"Do you want me to butt out, sir? If I do, I'll miss out on vital information that could move our cases forward. One of the murdered girls worked at that club, I'm sure of it."

"How sure?"

"She was wearing one of their work uniforms and we found her body within inches of Agnes Moore's — the one who tried to help the girls."

"I doubt that's compelling enough evidence. You need the dead girl's identity and positive proof she worked in that club. Get that and I'll lobby the ACC myself, and make sure you get all the interviews you require."

Harding was on her side after all. That was all Rachel needed to hear. "Thank you, sir. I was beginning to think you were firmly on Kenton's side."

"No, Rachel. It might not look like it, but I've always put my people first." He fell silent. "I'm ill, Rachel. I have neither the energy nor the resolve I used to have."

This was unexpected news. Harding's behaviour had certainly changed, but Rachel had put it down to stress.

"I have prostate cancer. It's quite advanced, they tell me."

The words hung between them. Rachel had no idea how to respond. Finally she said, "But you are having treatment?"

"Yes, I start the nasty stuff next week. It'll take me a few weeks to recuperate, and then I plan to retire."

"I'm sorry, sir. I had no idea."

"Kindly keep this to yourself for now. Sympathy is all very well, but I still have the department to run and I prefer to continue as normal."

Rachel went back to the incident room to ring Jude. She should have guessed there was something up with Harding, he'd not been himself for a while. He didn't want people to know, so that's how it would be.

"Hi, Jude. Any luck with the familial match on Anita Darwin and our unknown?"

"Later today, I promise," Jude said. "Are you okay? I heard about what happened yesterday."

"I'm fine, Jude. Well, I'm getting on with the job, which works for me."

"Don't push your luck. PTSD is a very real thing, and I wouldn't like to see you laid low for want of a few days with your feet up."

Rachel wasn't getting into that now. When were people going to stop telling her to take time off? "We sent a laptop over to digital forensics yesterday. It came from Leo's club in town. Do you know if they've processed it yet?"

"I'll chase them and have the data emailed over. Take care, Rachel. Work is great at stopping the cogs turning, but you had a shock yesterday. A bit of time off wouldn't hurt."

"You know me, Jude, a glutton for punishment. You still have the dead man's ring. Process it anyway, would you? Any trace of Agnes Moore's DNA let me know."

"I was in the middle of processing Akerman's clothing and samples when Kenton's mob stepped in," Jude said. "But after our little chat, I carried on. Akerman bit his assailant. I found traces of blood in his mouth. The DNA is a match for Danulescu's, which is on file."

"That proves what we thought. Thanks, Jude."

"Not that it helps much now — the man is dead. Please consider your own well-being, Rachel. You can only push yourself so far."

Rachel sighed inwardly. This would be the norm for the next few days. She'd better get used to it. As her colleagues heard what had happened, they'd all be urging her to take time off. Most people would take their advice, but Rachel wasn't most people. She needed to work. Resting would have to wait.

"Ruby's awake," Elwyn called out to her. "The doctor reckons she'll be up to talking later today. Fancy a trip to the MRI?"

Rachel nodded. "We'll go after I've spoken to the girls. I don't want Kenton beating us to it. The Blakes, Amy. Anything?"

"I'm still digging, ma'am."

"Get a warrant and we'll look into his finances while we're at it. That might give us something."

"Sure you're up for this?" Elwyn said. "Interviewing those girls could get messy."

"Elwyn, I'm coping fine. Don't keep on about it."

CHAPTER TWENTY-EIGHT

Amy had got everything set up in one of the soft interview rooms. The interpreter was waiting.

"Elwyn, did yesterday's search of the club throw anything up?" Rachel asked.

He shook his head. "No, the place was clean. No drugs, and no stash of money, other than the previous night's takings. I didn't think much of the girl's accommodation, though. I wouldn't keep a dog in those rooms."

"Did you find any employment records?"

"Nothing. As you know, we brought in a laptop from the office there. Digital forensics are still working on it."

"Hope the girls give us something useful," she said. "They must have seen things, suspicious goings-on."

Elwyn looked dubious. "But will they talk to you?"

Rachel left the incident room and went downstairs to the interview room. She wanted a quick word with Amy before they got started.

"We go easy," she said. "No losing it. Despite the drug taking and whatever else they might have done, these girls aren't criminals. They're scared. Bad as it was, we've just dragged them away from the only place they knew. We need to gain their trust, convince them that they won't be going back to that life. They're free."

Entering the room, Rachel saw how young the girls were. Some weren't even Megan's age. Her heart went out to them. She smiled and sat down. "Hello. My name's Rachel and this is Amy. We want to talk to you about how we can help."

None of them looked very impressed. "You can help by letting us go," one of them said. "You don't know what it's like — he'll kill us for this."

"If you're talking about Danulescu, he can't hurt anyone anymore."

"You don't know that. He knows people, and you can't hold him forever."

Should she tell them that he was dead? It would most likely only scare them further. "You'll have to trust me on this — Danulescu can't hurt you."

"Do we have to stay here? Are we under arrest?" another girl asked.

"What's your name?" Rachel asked her.

The girl averted her eyes and said nothing.

"No harm will come to you. You're not in any trouble. You can talk freely. I want you to trust me," Rachel said.

"If you really want to help, then let us go. Mrs Blake will want us at the club for opening time."

Rachel shook her head. "Mrs Blake has been arrested. She's not going anywhere. If you want to stay safe, speak to us."

The four girls fell silent, exchanging furtive looks — wondering, no doubt who, if any of them, would speak up first.

"He said the work would pay well, that there'd be tips and a nice place to stay," one of them said finally. "But he was lying!"

"Danulescu?"

The girl nodded.

She had a good command of English, so Rachel directed her questions at her. "Tell me your name — just your first name if that makes you feel more comfortable." Rachel smiled.

After a moment or two, the girl said, "Marsela."

"How old are you, Marsela?"

"Sixteen."

"Where do you come from?"

"Albania."

"How did you get to the UK?" Rachel asked.

"Danulescu brought me, along with the others. He said there was work, that we'd be able to save and have a good life."

Rachel nodded. "Can you tell us how long you've been working at that club?"

"Nearly a year," the girl said, looking down.

"Danulescu was breaking the law," Amy said. "You're far too young to be working in a club, or any bar. Couldn't you tell him, or the Blakes, that you wanted to leave?"

"He said no one could leave until they'd paid off their debt. He charged us all for the transport here. It was hundreds of euros. There is no way we can ever pay it off." She spread her hands.

The other girls were nodding. It was the same story with all of them.

One of the girls was English. She said her name was Anna. Rachel wondered what her story was.

"My mum got a new bloke. He were drunk most of the time and threw me out. I had nowhere to go. Mum wasn't bothered — most days she was off her head on coke. I came into the city but it was hard on the streets. I never felt safe, not even in the hostels. One day I met this older lad called Nicu. He took me to see Danulescu, and he gave me the job."

Nicu again! That young man popped up everywhere. "Where do you live, Anna?" Rachel asked.

"All of us live at the club. In the attic. They don't like us going out," Anna said.

The girl sitting next to Anna nudged her.

"What is it?" Rachel asked.

After a pause, Anna spoke up. "They keep us prisoners. When we've finished in the bar, we're all locked in one room, the lot of us." She looked away. "And then there's the men."

"What men?" Amy asked her.

"Them men Danulescu brings. We're nothing but prostitutes, except that we don't see any of the money."

"Danulescu pimps you out as prostitutes?" Amy asked, astonished.

"Yes."

"Do you know any of these men?" asked Rachel.

Anna shook her head. "I've said enough. Things won't go well for us if Mrs Blake finds out I've spoken to you."

"You've been very brave," Rachel said. "And I can assure you that none of you will be going back to that club. You won't have to see Mrs Blake again. We will find all of you a safe place to live."

"Is it just you four work in Leo's?" asked Amy.

"We're the only ones that was there that morning you raided the place," Anna said. "The other girls were working somewhere else."

"Do you know where?" asked Rachel.

"No. They only let the trusted ones go there," Anna said.

"Some girls get sold." All eyes turned to the girl who had just spoken. "I only found that out last week. I came to this country with a friend. She disappeared, and I think that's what happened to her."

"What was your friend's name?" Rachel asked.

"Elira."

"When did you see her last?" Amy asked.

"At least a month ago. Elira was pretty, with long blonde hair. Men liked her. Danulescu will have got a lot of money for her."

Just the thought of this was unbearable. Somewhere out there was a young, frightened girl who probably didn't have much English, a girl with nowhere to turn.

"I'm going to speak to some colleagues who have more experience in this sort of thing than I do," Rachel said. "They

172

know what you must do if you want to stay in the UK. Or if you'd prefer to go home, they can arrange that too."

* * *

The interview was over.

Amy looked shaken. "Those girls have been through hell," she said.

Rachel saw from her expression that the young DC was genuinely shocked. "Take comfort in the knowledge that we've put a stop to it — at least where those involved with the Blakes are concerned," she said. "All their clubs will be visited and the girls helped. We have social services specialists on the case. They will look after them until their future becomes a bit clearer."

"D'you reckon they know much more about who else is involved?" Amy asked.

Rachel shook her head. "I doubt it. They'd see plenty of people come and go in that club, but they'd have no idea who was who."

"What about those other poor girls they mentioned? Do we stand any chance of finding them? This is huge, isn't it?" Amy's voice was trembling. She was truly upset.

"We'll do what we can," Rachel said. "We'll pass all the information on to the relevant department, but for now, that's it."

Back in the incident room, Jonny was waiting for her. "Ma'am, DI Knight has asked if he can have a word."

"Did he say what about?" Rachel asked.

"No, but he said you might be interested."

"If it's not relevant to our current case then it'll have to wait. I'll speak to him later. Have we got Agnes's phone data through yet?" she called over to Stella.

"I'll give them a nudge."

"Anything on the white van, Jonny? Have we managed to track it on CCTV?"

"Only so far. It stops next to Agnes and we presume picks her up. Then the cameras spot it on John Dalton Street.

173

It spends some time just riding round and round, and it finally disappears over towards Media City."

"There are cameras down there," Rachel said.

"I said towards. I don't think it went there. There is a gap of roughly an hour when it's off the radar. It could have parked up somewhere. The next sighting is along Ashton Old Road, just before it stops at the building site. I've got the stills — we're definitely looking at the same van."

"They're emailing me the data from Agnes's phone now, ma'am," Stella confirmed. "They've got people off sick, which is why it took so long."

"It's a long shot, but we might get something." Rachel waited while Stella printed off the data and then sat down to study it. She didn't have a lot of time, there was still Ruby to speak to.

"There are a lot of different numbers here. Amy, would you match up the ones that belong to her sister and colleagues? Then we'll see what we're left with."

CHAPTER TWENTY-NINE

Ruby was by herself in a room off the main ward. A uniformed officer stood in the corridor outside, watching the people going past.

"There's been no visitors, ma'am," he told Rachel.

Good, they'd got here before Kenton. Rachel and Elwyn went in.

Deathly pale, Ruby was breathing through an oxygen mask.

Rachel smiled at her. "Hello, Ruby. Are you up for visitors?"

"I've seen you before," Ruby said hoarsely. "You're police. Why've you come here? I haven't done anything wrong." She was overwhelmed by a fit of coughing.

Rachel waited while she got her breath back and offered her a sip of water. "It's a good job you went to Mavis. She got you here just in time."

"I was desperate. I've never been so ill. I didn't know life on the streets would be so hard."

"Ruby, we need your help," Rachel said, getting down to business. "You're not in any trouble, and I promise that if there's someone threatening your life, we'll protect you."

"That's easy for you to say, but you don't know these people. Just being seen with you could get me killed."

"We're investigating the murder of Agnes Moore. You knew her. Remember we met? Outside the health centre. You asked about Agnes."

"I did know her, but not that well. Agnes was a nurse at the health centre. I went to her with a problem and she sorted me out. When I visited her next, she offered to help me get away from that club."

"How was she going to do that?" Rachel asked.

"She said she could get me a place to stay and a different job."

"That was a good thing, wasn't it?" Elwyn said.

"Depends on how you look at it."

"Did Agnes tell you what sort of job she had in mind, or where you'd be living?" Rachel asked.

"She never told me the details." Ruby turned her head aside and began coughing again.

Ruby was hiding something. But what?

"Did Agnes help other girls, Ruby?" Elwyn asked.

"I don't know. We didn't talk about anyone else."

Ruby flushed — she was lying.

"Did you and Agnes get on?"

The girl obviously wasn't finding this easy. When she spoke about Agnes, her voice became flat, toneless.

"She was okay so long as you stuck to the rules. Agnes liked rules. But cross her and she could lose it. Agnes was no saint. She'd help, but at a cost. She did nothing for free."

"What d'you mean, Ruby? What did she want in return? She must have known you had no money. That was why you went to her for help."

"You have no idea what Agnes was really like. Everyone thinks she was an angel, but she was selfish, grasping. She'd have sold her own mother if she thought it would turn a profit!"

Rachel was taken aback. This wasn't her impression of Agnes. Ruby's outburst had brought on an enormous fit of coughing. Rachel tapped her foot. She didn't want to push the girl too hard, but how long would it be before Kenton showed his face and took over?

"When we uncovered Agnes's body, we also found the body of a girl. She was wearing a pink outfit, the same as you had on that day. We think she worked at the club too. Have you any idea who she was?" Rachel asked.

"Sorry, no."

"We think she might have been called Jess. Does that ring any bells?"

"I told you, no.

The coughing worsened until Ruby seemed close to vomiting. Rachel pressed the button to summon a nurse.

"Go away," Ruby sobbed. "I don't know any more. Stop hassling me."

"We'll talk again when you're a bit better," Rachel said. "I need you to tell me about Nicu Bogdan and the Blakes." The girl's eyes widened. She looked terrified. "Don't worry, you're quite safe in here. I've left an officer on guard."

Out in the corridor, Rachel had a quick word with the PC. "Anyone visits, ring me at the station, and don't let her go anywhere. I have a sneaky suspicion that she'll try to run the minute she's well enough." Then she and Elwyn took the stairs to the exit.

"She won't run, will she? Surely she wouldn't be so stupid?" Elwyn asked.

"She's afraid of something, or someone. She didn't seem to like Agnes much either, which wasn't the impression I got of her. I thought Agnes was a kind woman who tried to help those who needed it."

"Ruby was being very guarded," Elwyn said. "Who knows what she really thinks? We'll see if things change when she recovers. I note you didn't push it about Nicu."

"I think that's who she is afraid of. She's been living on the streets, desperately trying to hide. But why? What has she done, or know, that's made her so afraid?"

"She ran for a reason, Rachel. And it's all bound up with that club and the people who work there."

* * *

Back at the station, Jude was waiting for her. "For you!" She held out a bottle of Pinot Noir wine. Rachel's favourite. "Unwind with a glass in front of the telly tonight and just vegetate."

"Tempting, Jude, but it's unlikely I'll get the chance. Great wine though, and thanks." Rachel smiled. How thoughtful of her.

"The DNA from Anita Darwin is a familial match to your unknown girl," Jude announced.

"That means we have her identity at last. The girl is Jess Darwin, Anita's granddaughter."

"Digital forensics are still working on the laptop. According to Len, there's plenty of interesting stuff on it — accounts, bank details, the lot."

Len Bradley was good at his job. If the information was there, encrypted or not, he'd extract it.

"He'll let you have his report as soon as. But he sent this with me." Jude handed over a printout, a list of names. "All girls, just first names and dates. Most of them are foreign."

Rachel scanned the list. She saw two of the girls she'd already spoken to, as well as Jess. But the list ran into pages. Hundreds of trafficked girls had passed through the Blakes' club.

"This is what passes for employee records, I suppose. No wages, nothing saying where they came from, or even their surnames." She looked across at Stella. "Would you check if Salford are still holding Leonora Blake? I wouldn't mind a word."

"Don Akerman was shot with a bullet from a Glock," Jude said. "The gun used to kill the others was a different make. We haven't finished our tests on the bodies of Agnes and Jess yet. If I get anything else, I'll be in touch."

So Rachel finally had her ID, plus proof that the dead girl worked in Leo's. Time for another word with Harding.

* * *

Nicu Bogdan had scoured the streets of the city but had found no sign of her. Just like that, Ruby had disappeared in a puff of smoke. Well, all that would cut no ice with the boss. Nicu was running out of time. He'd been given a deadline. Miss it and it'd be his life at risk. Time to dish out some serious aggro.

His first stop was the hostel on Ashton Old Road. Nicu turned up at lunchtime with a bunch of thugs, intent on causing havoc. The woman who ran the place would talk or suffer the consequences. His first act was to take a baseball bat to the counter, sending food, dishes and everything else flying to the floor. Amid screams, he and his gang set about wrecking the place.

"It'll be someone's head next!" He shrieked, sending everyone running for cover. "Where is she? Where's Ruby? Who's hiding the bitch?"

"She's not here." Shaken but defiant, Mavis Smithson faced him. "So you can take your bunch of villains and do one."

Nicu glared at her, bat in hand. "I'll crack your skull open if you don't tell me. She comes in here. You feed her. Last chance — speak up woman!" He shook the bat.

"She's sick. An ambulance took her last night. Now bugger off and leave us in peace. Come back and it'll be the police sorting you."

"How sick?" The bat fell to his side.

"How should I know? I'm no nurse. I just dish out soup and sandwiches."

She was telling the truth, she had to be. Cursing, Nicu and his thugs left, swinging their bats. "Manchester Royal Infirmary next," Nicu said. "But I'll go alone. Less chance of being picked up that way. The cops don't know me. I'll borrow a white coat and no one will be any the wiser." He smiled. "Very soon, boys, I'll get that bitch, and then it's job done."

CHAPTER THIRTY

Rachel was pleased with herself. Harding had spoken to Kenton and had arranged for her to sit in on the interview with Leonora Blake at Salford. It was scheduled for three that afternoon.

"The loving husband hasn't shown his face," she told the team. "Kenton's missed a trick there. My gut instinct is rarely wrong, and it's telling me Blake is behind it all. Our not so friendly DCI must be tearing his hair out searching for him. Problem is, the Blakes own so much property he could be anywhere."

"We have a list of most of it," Elwyn said.

"Might be prudent to give them the once over. Let me know if you turn up anything."

Jonny hastened in, panting. "Ma'am. There's been a ruck at the hostel. Mavis says four blokes turned up looking for Ruby and wrecked the place. Mavis didn't recognise any of them, but the ringleader had a foreign accent."

That was all they needed. "Could have been Nicu Bogdan," Rachel said. "He's another one we need to find in a hurry. Was anyone hurt?"

"Thankfully no, but Mavis was forced to tell them that Ruby was ill and had been carted off in an ambulance. It won't take them long to find where she is."

"Double up on the watch. We can't risk anything happening to Ruby. She's an important witness, and she's in our care."

Rachel picked up the list of girls' names and went to her office to get ready for the drive to Salford. She couldn't wait to hear Leonora Blake try and talk her way out of this one.

* * *

The station in Salford was a large, rambling building on the ring road. It wasn't far from Rachel's own station but the traffic was heavy and the going slow. She made it with only minutes to spare.

"Her solicitor is one of the top men from a reputable firm in town," Kenton said. "She is insisting she knows nothing about trafficking, and that her husband sourced and hired the girls without consulting her."

"She's lying. She had to know. Did you see where those poor girls were made to live? I wouldn't keep an animal in that accommodation. She must have known what it was like."

"My team will need to speak to the four girls you brought in." Rachel scowled. "We'll be gentle," he insisted, "they'll be under no pressure. But if we're to keep Mrs Blake in custody, we need all the evidence they can give us."

"Speaking of which, this might come in useful." Rachel handed him a copy of the list of girls' names. "It was on a laptop from the office at the club. There were no employment records, just this."

"Where is the laptop now?"

"Digital forensics have it. There could well be further stuff on there that will help."

Kenton and Rachel stopped for a moment outside the door to the interview room. "Let me do the talking," he said, "unless there is some burning issue you need to bring up."

This was no time to start arguing. Rachel simply nodded, silently determined to have her say, Kenton or no Kenton.

Introductions for the tape out of the way, Kenton launched into the interrogation. Leonora refused to answer every one of them, responding to each with a "no comment."

Rachel had heard enough. The woman was playing games. It was about time she knew the score. As soon as Kenton fell silent, she cut in with, "Aren't you concerned about your husband, Mrs Blake? If I was you, I'd be very worried indeed. I'd be asking myself why he hasn't come forward to offer his support. But perhaps he can't. There are some dangerous people out there. His life could be in danger." She gave Leonora a moment to consider this. "Are you aware that Danulescu has been killed? Shot through the head by an unknown sniper."

This obviously shook Leonora. She turned pale. "When did this happen?"

"Sorry, but we're the ones asking the questions," Kenton told her.

"Interesting that you are concerned about Danulescu's death," Rachel said. "Are you maybe worried that your husband has gone too far?"

"Ronan wouldn't kill anyone!" Leonora shouted. "You've got this all wrong."

Rachel leaned back in her chair and smiled. "I doubt that very much. But do feel free to put us right, Mrs Blake. I would hate to see an innocent man brought to book over something he didn't do."

"Okay, I admit Ronan is mixed up in it, but he is not the one running the enterprise."

"You make it sound like a business. Well, it's a long way from being that," Rachel retorted. "You and your husband are involved in human trafficking." She allowed this too to sink in. "You keep those girls half-starved and feed them dope to ensure they stay in line."

"You can't prove any of this." Leonora looked at her solicitor. "Not against me, anyway."

"So, if not you, tell me who is to blame. These are appalling crimes, and someone has to pay."

"Not me, and not Ronan," Leonora insisted. "We were coerced."

This made Rachel laugh. No way could she imagine anyone having that much power over those two.

"You're lying. It's written all over your face. We've got the girls and they're talking to us. In fact, we can barely shut them up. Why not do the right thing and tell us what you know?"

Leonora Blake shook her head. "Not with a sniper on the loose. I speak to you and I'll be signing my own death warrant." She dabbed at her eyes.

"Do you know a girl called Jess Darwin?" Rachel asked, ignoring Leonora's theatrics.

"Never heard of her."

"Maybe you don't know any of the girls' names. Perhaps there are just too many to be bothered learning them. You bring them into the country, work them like dogs for a while and then sell them on. That's what happens, isn't it?"

"You are making this up to upset me." Leonora turned to Kenton. "Is she telling the truth about Danulescu? Is he really dead?"

"Mrs Blake, we're simply trying to get to the truth," Kenton told her, evading the question. "All we want is to stop the trafficking of young girls and arrest whoever is involved. If you tell us what you know, things could get a lot easier."

Rachel gave him a nudge in the ribs. That sounded suspiciously like the offer of a deal, perhaps the one he'd offered Danulescu. Leonora gives him evidence of her husband's guilt, possibly even tells him where Ronan is hiding, and she disappears off to lead a new life. Rachel wasn't having any of it. The Blakes deserved everything the law could throw at them.

Kenton stood up. "We'll leave it for now."

Just as well. Rachel was about to say something she might regret. Kenton was a piece of work. There was no way he was getting away with it.

Out in the corridor, though, she gave it to him. "I'm not stupid. I worked out where that was going. You can't cut a deal with that woman. She's evil. Jess worked for the Blakes, and now she's dead. Goodness knows how many more they've killed."

"You have no proof that the Blakes killed this girl, or any of the others."

"But it's looking highly likely. I told you our cases were linked. I've got two bodies, well, four if you count Akerman and Danulescu. The one thing linking them all is that club and the Blakes."

Kenton ignored all this. "You got her talking, and that helped. But your involvement with Leonora Blake is now at an end."

"What are you frightened of?" Rachel shot back. "That I'll crack this case before you? Steal your thunder? Didn't you hear what I said? I have four murder victims. Four. That woman knows what happened, I'd stake my job on it."

"I wouldn't if I were you," Kenton said. "Come to my office, have a mug of coffee and calm down before you say something you might regret."

The coffee sounded okay, but Rachel couldn't promise about the calm. The man was a moron. Almost everything he said wound her up.

His office was a poky room on the third floor with a view of the car park and the River Irwell beyond. She sat down and waited while he made the coffee.

Neither spoke, the only noise was that of the kettle and the chink of crockery. Rachel watched him, trying to work out what his problem was. Was it women, she wondered? Women in senior positions? He certainly didn't like sharing information. Was it just that he didn't like her?

He handed her a mug and sat down facing her. "How well do you know Jed McAteer?"

Where had that come from? The unexpected question threw her for a moment. "I'm not sure what you're getting at."

"It's a simple enough question. You went to an event at an apartment of his the other night. From the way you greeted each other, it was presumed you were friends."

Someone had been watching and had reported back to Kenton. But, who? More to the point, why? Well, she had no hesitation in fabricating a story, not where Kenton was concerned. "I attended the event with another officer on my team. It was on the back of the case we're investigating. McAteer had made such a fuss about his building site being out of bounds while we recovered the bodies that he wanted to make amends, and so he gave us invitations to the opening bash."

He nodded. "Sounds plausible."

"That's because it's the truth! I don't know what you're trying to get at, Kenton, but why not save us both all this pussy-footing around and just spit out whatever you really want to say?"

"You've got me all wrong. I was interested, that's all. It is possible that you can help me with something."

Rachel gave him a filthy look. "Why would I want to do that? You do little or nothing to help with my case. I had to get Harding to step in just so I could be here today. I've had enough. But be warned. If my team find Blake first, it will be you waiting your turn."

Rachel slammed the mug down, spilling coffee on his desk, and stormed out. Stuff the bloody interview. Kenton could go to hell!

The truth was, he had her rattled. Why had Kenton brought up McAteer? Sure, Jed knew the Blakes, but so did half of Manchester. That wasn't a good enough reason, and he'd know about the building site and the problems with the search. No, this was about something else. Rachel could only hope that Kenton got involved in the present case and let it drop.

CHAPTER THIRTY-ONE

Dressed in a set of green scrubs with a fake ID badge, Nicu Bogdan entered the MRI. He'd no idea where Ruby was in this vast hospital, but if she'd been taken ill, not broken anything or been injured, the chances were she was on a medical ward.

"Dr Jameson?" a nurse asked as he exited the lift.

He smiled at her. "He's running late. I'm his right hand today, but this is my first time in the hospital and I keep getting lost."

"Happens to us all, love. Wait for him over there by the main desk."

"Actually, I wouldn't mind earning myself some brownie points. Do you know where I can find a Ruby Wood?"

She smiled. "Our little runaway. She's down that corridor on the right, in the side room at the bottom."

"Thanks."

Piece of cake. People were so gullible. He picked up a random file off the desk and, casually flicking through it, turned into the corridor. Nicu spotted the two uniforms at the door to Ruby's room. He nodded at them and went in, closing the door behind him.

He stood over the bed. "Not a word, or you're dead."

There was a knock at the door. "Sorry, sir, but we have to keep the young lady in our sights at all times."

"Sorry, didn't realise." He smiled at them.

Nicu picked up the chart from the end of her bed and whispered in her ear, "Time's up, Ruby. You were warned."

"I haven't said nowt. I'm no threat to you."

"Not what the boss thinks. Take this, and hide it well. You will say nothing about my little visit or things will not go well for you." Pretending to check her oxygen machine, he slipped her a mobile phone. "I'll be in touch."

* * *

Rachel returned to the station in a foul mood. Kenton had really pissed her off. His bringing up Jed like that was upsetting, but it had also made her curious. Still, there were more pressing matters to think about now.

She gathered the team together. They needed to look at what they'd got, which wasn't enough to present to the CPS.

"We still haven't identified Agnes and Jess's killer. Time's passing and we haven't got a thing." She looked at each of her team in turn. "Come on, shape up. We have to find who killed them. Take another look at what we've got and if necessary, go and speak to the people who knew Agnes again."

A groan went round the room. They were working hard, but just weren't getting the breaks.

"We know that Danulescu killed Akerman," Rachel said. "Akerman bit the Romanian and we have a positive DNA match. But Danulescu is dead, so we can't pursue that one."

"Are we going with Danulescu killing Agnes and Jess?" Amy asked.

"Unlikely. It was a different bullet for starters, came from a Glock and not an old army weapon like the others. Then there was the amount of violence used," Rachel added.

"Perhaps Agnes got too close to what Blake was up to and visited the club. Possibly she even tackled him. He couldn't risk her speaking to us, so he had her killed," Elwyn suggested.

It was a good theory, but she had her reservations. "I don't see Blake having anyone killed with a gun that's a relic from seventy years ago. Human trafficking is organised crime. He must have access to high-powered modern weapons."

The team fell quiet. The expression on their faces said Rachel was right. Blake might be responsible for Danulescu and in turn, Akerman, but not Agnes and Jess.

"Do we have any further info on Blake? Who he was until twenty years ago will do for starters."

"I've been doing the research on that, ma'am, but it's tricky. I've narrowed it down to three possibles." Amy handed Rachel the paperwork. She recognised one of them, Jamie Chisnall, and the name immediately rang warning bells. Years ago, he'd been a friend of Jed's. He and Jamie had embarked on a life of crime together. This had to be Ronan Blake. Jed must have recognised him, but chosen not to tell her about his change of identity.

"Pull the record on Chisnall," she told Amy, with no further explanation.

"We are still searching Blake's properties, ma'am," Jonny said. "A lot of them are empty, but so far there's no sign of him."

"Make sure all the airports, ports and any other borders are made aware," Rachel said.

"Already done, but it's thrown up nothing so far."

Rachel stared at the incident board. She'd pinned up the image of Blake at the top, with the names Danulescu, Nicu Bogdan and Leonora beneath it. But where did Akerman, Agnes and Jess fit in? She picked up the phone. A quick word with Jude was needed.

"Have you managed to get anything from Danulescu's ring yet?"

"Give me until the end of the day. We did find blood — faint traces between the stone and the mount. Something else that might interest you, I've been giving the clothing

Agnes and the girl were wearing the once over. Agnes's has those fibreglass fibres on it, but we did find something else." She paused. Rachel could hear her speaking to one of the lab technicians.

"Go on, Jude, what did you find?"

"Flakes."

"Flakes?" Rachel thought of breakfast cereal.

"It could be that whoever killed them both suffers with the skin condition, psoriasis."

"That causes flaky skin?"

"Very much so. It's like a much worse version of eczema."

"Can you get DNA from these flakes?"

"It'll take time and it'll cost, but yes."

"Do it, Jude. We need all the evidence we can get."

Rachel wrote this new snippet on the incident board. Given the little they had, it was significant.

"Listen up," she called to the team. "We've all been out, spoken to a lot of people. Have any of you noticed anyone with a skin condition?" There was a general shaking of heads. "Keep it in mind. Look up a skin condition called psoriasis, find someone involved in this who has it, and they could be our killer." She wrote 'psoriasis' on the board.

"DI Knight's asked if he can have a word, ma'am," Jonny told her. "It's a couple he's been dealing with. He thinks they may be of more interest to you."

"What couple?"

"They came in the other day and made a complaint. Said it was a delicate matter. They reckon they're the victims of some scam."

"Can't Knight deal with it?"

Jonny shrugged. "He says not."

This was no time to be hand-holding detectives from other teams. "I'll speak to him later."

"Are we passing on the info about Blake's true identity to Kenton?" Elwyn asked her.

"No, we're not. He can do his own digging. He gives us nowt!"

189

Elwyn grinned. "You really don't like him, do you?"

"He is going to do a deal with Leonora. I was in that interview, I saw the way it was heading. What sort of detective gets the lowdown on one villain by letting another walk free? He needs to get out there, get the evidence and do his bloody job properly."

Rachel went to her office. She made a mug of tea and started to take another look at the statements they'd gathered. No one had said very much — certainly nothing helpful. Akerman, Danulescu, even Ruby, they had all been too frightened to talk to her. Ronan Blake had some reach. But where was he now? Hiding in one of his properties? Or had he skipped the country already? He had to have contacts abroad, Romania and Albania in particular.

Elwyn interrupted her ruminations. "We've just had a call, Rachel, and you're not going to like it."

She looked up from the pile of statements. "Oh?"

"They've found Ronan Blake."

She smiled. "What's not to like about that?"

"He's dead."

CHAPTER THIRTY-TWO

The body of Jamie Chisnall, alias Ronan Blake, was found in an empty flat in Ardwick. The block was dilapidated, most of the tenants having moved out after it had been earmarked for demolition. The immediate area was run down and sparsely populated so it was unlikely there'd be any witnesses, but they had to go through the motions anyway.

On hearing the news, Rachel immediately arranged for Jude to meet them at the flat. By the time she and Elwyn arrived, Jude had already done an initial assessment.

"He was killed outright, a single shot to the head. From the angle of entry, I reckon that he was standing here, by the window, and that the shot came from that direction." She pointed.

"There's another block across there. Get your people to take a look," Rachel said.

"Already on it," Jude said.

"It looks as if he was holed up here," Elwyn said. "Not many home comforts but it's the sort of place no one comes looking."

"Except us." Rachel smiled. "Who found him?"

"That young PC over there," Jude replied. "It's his first body, hence the vomit in the hallway."

Dr Colin Butterfield had made his initial examination. "There are no other wounds that I can see. Damn good shot, mind you. He hit his head on the wall as he fell, but that's all I can see at this time."

"You can take him away," Rachel said. She turned to Elwyn. "It wasn't just us Blake was hiding from, which trashes my theory that Blake was running the trafficking gang."

"He might have been. Not even gang leaders are immune from violence. Perhaps he crossed someone, maybe another Romanian like Danulescu. They're a hard bunch. Given what's happened — his wife being arrested — Blake might have ceased to be useful."

"I don't think so, not with the number of clubs he owns. He was tried and tested. I don't like this, Elwyn. This smacks of someone clearing up prior to disappearing."

The two detectives left the flat, crossing the road and a patch of rough ground to reach the block the shot supposedly came from. Rachel could see Jude's people working several floors up.

"There's no lift," Elwyn said.

"Wouldn't use one in a place like this anyway. You could be stuck in it for months before it got fixed." They trudged up the stairs.

"This is the spot." A CSI pointed to a window facing the block they had just come from. "Your shooter stood here."

"How d'you know?" asked Elwyn.

"He or she must have waited around for a while. They were eating a sandwich — see? There's crumbs on the floor. And muddy footprints."

It had been raining. That meant the killer possibly took a route across the same patch of rough ground as they had.

"Any CCTV, d'you reckon?" Rachel asked.

"I doubt it, but we'll look anyway."

Rachel peered at the floor. "Can you get anything from the crumbs or the shoe prints?"

"If there is saliva on the crumbs we'll get DNA. Might prove useful."

Then again, if the killer was an unknown Romanian, it wouldn't be any use at all. Rachel was at a loss. She was running out of suspects. She'd pinned such a lot on Blake being the head man. So who now?

Her ringtone interrupted her train of thought. It was Ruby, calling from a mobile. How in the world had she got hold of a phone? And why hadn't either of the uniforms discovered it?

"He's going to kill me," Ruby whispered. "You have to get me out of here. Nicu knows where I am and he'll be back to get me."

That hadn't taken him long. "Stay put. Do not leave that room. I will be with you soon."

Rachel turned to Elwyn. "Bloody idiots! That was Ruby. Nicu Bogdan has been to see her." She saw the look on Elwyn's face. "Yes, you heard right. Under the very noses of our uniforms, he walks in and leaves her with a mobile. No doubt he intends to contact her with instructions. We have to get over there, Elwyn, before she decides to leg it."

It was unlikely that Ruby was well enough to be transferred to a safe house. Instead they'd have to increase the watch and include an armed officer. They needed to stay on the ball. Ruby was an important witness.

Driving them to the hospital, Rachel heard her mobile ring again. "Get it for me, would you?" she asked Elwyn.

"It's your Megan. She asks if you're okay."

"Tell her I'm fine."

"She's coping in her usual way," Elwyn said. "Burying her head in the sand and pretending it didn't happen."

"I'm fine!" Rachel shouted. "Take no bloody notice of him."

After ending the call, Elwyn turned to her. "Megan's friend Shannon has had a text. There's an apartment free tonight, the same one as last time. She's texting you the details. Another night on the lash for a tenner."

"Arranged by Nicu, no doubt. We can't miss this opportunity, Elwyn. He always turns up to collect the money. We'll have to set things up and wait for him."

"We can't attempt to bring him in if there's any chance he's armed. If he's texted Shannon, loads of kids will know by now. The place will be packed."

"We'll make sure we've got the apartment secure. When they turn up, we'll direct them elsewhere."

"It's risky. For all we know, Nicu could be our shooter."

* * *

Within minutes, Rachel and Elwyn were at the hospital. The two uniforms were still outside the room, oblivious to what had happened.

Rachel launched into them. "Why not try doing your jobs? He was here, the bloke we're looking for. You let him get to her. You're lucky she's not dead!"

"The DCI is not best pleased. He left Ruby a mobile and she used it to ring us," Elwyn added.

Leaving Elwyn to thrash out security procedures with the uniforms, Rachel went in to speak to the girl.

"You did the right thing in ringing me, Ruby. How did he get to you? Why didn't they spot him?" She nodded to the door.

"He was dressed just like a doctor. The cops out there had no idea. And I couldn't do a thing. He'd have killed me on the spot."

Rachel looked at the girl. She was still pale and very thin, her arms were like sticks. Her once vivid pink hair was showing at least an inch of dark roots. "I want to help you, Ruby, but in turn you've got to help me. Why are you so afraid of Nicu?"

"Because I know something," Ruby said flatly.

"Will you tell me what that is?" asked Rachel.

"Vasile liked me, he tried to keep me safe, then, one night when there was just the two of us he got drunk and high on coke. I looked at his phone, the special one he uses for work. I knew it was a risk but I wanted some leverage. He caught me and went ballistic. There were only a few contacts on it, but I remembered who they were."

"Was Ronan Blake one?"

"Yes, he was there. He ran the club, Leo's. I worked there for a bit. Nicu hated him. I think he had the hots for Ronan's wife."

"Who else did you see, Ruby?"

"Leo, Nicu and Mac."

CHAPTER THIRTY-THREE

With the new procedures in place, Rachel and Elwyn left Ruby to get some rest. "From now on, she'll be treated by a small team, all of them known to our people. No one else will be allowed to go into that room."

"Did she tell you anything?" Elwyn asked.

"Nothing that helps." Rachel hesitated slightly. Elwyn had been outside with the uniforms when Ruby gave her the names. "Which is a shame, because now we're short of a suspect for head man."

Rachel took a deep breath. She shouldn't be doing this. Elwyn and the team had every right to know what she'd just been told. Leo, Nicu — and Mac. Jed McAteer had always been known as Mac. He had to be in the frame. She could not protect him now. She shouldn't protect him.

"What about Leonora? We thought her husband was calling the shots, but perhaps we were wrong. She's a bright lady. I wouldn't put anything past her," Elwyn said.

Rachel had asked Elwyn to drive — her head was hammering, and her mind was in turmoil. She closed her eyes. If only that was the case. She'd have given anything for it to be Leonora, but it wasn't. Soon Ruby would recover. She'd make a statement, and so would Nicu once they had him in custody. Jed McAteer's fate would be sealed. Rachel tried to put it together. Had the clues been there all along? Agnes and Jess were found on his land. He'd been at the party in the bar that night, and he knew the Blakes. Plus, he was an old friend of Jamie Chisnall — Blake's former persona. But people trafficking? Rachel couldn't believe Jed would sink so low.

"Who d'you reckon for tonight?" she asked.

"Me, Jonny and a load of uniforms. Plus armed response, given he could be carrying a weapon."

"Hey, what about me?" Rachel nudged him. "You're not having all the fun, DS Pryce. We've been chasing this little toerag for days now. He could be in the frame for Agnes and Jess. He's bound to have known Jess too, since she worked at the club."

"It might be an idea for you to get some rest," Elwyn said.

"Absolutely not. When my officers put themselves on the line, it's only fair that I join them."

Elwyn sighed. "Okay, have it your way. Regardless of what I say, you'll end up doing as you please."

* * *

Back at the station, Rachel gathered the team and they discussed the plan for later. "Jonny — you, Elwyn and half a dozen uniformed officers. Armed response is going to be on standby just in case." She double-checked the address on her mobile. "The apartment is on floor twenty-one, number ten. It's accessed from the lift along a corridor with tinted glass windows. We'll position our people inside, out of sight. She checked her watch. "Time's moving on. It's already turned four, and we should get ready. The apartment will be free from seven onwards. Once our people are in position, text me."

Rachel was running on adrenalin — the only thing that was keeping her going. Elwyn was right, the sensible option would be an early night, but she needed to be there when Nicu was apprehended. He'd talk and when he did, Jed would be top of the suspect list. And then?

Seated behind her desk with a mug of strong coffee, Rachel thought back to her conversation with Kenton. He'd asked her about Jed. She'd swerved that one by blabbing on about the party in the bar, but was Kenton convinced? If he already suspected Jed, had he done his research? More to the point, did he know the truth about Jed and her?

It was time for a full and frank discussion with the man.

* * *

DCI Mark Kenton was only too happy to come to Rachel's office, once she told him what it was about.

"Over the last year or so, McAteer has become something of a pet project of mine," he began.

Rachel shook her head. "You need to get out more."

"You find that amusing, do you, Rachel? Believe me, it's not. That man is evil. I'm not taken in by the reformed businessman act. That's just not McAteer. What d'you think? You know him better than me. You've known McAteer for years, haven't you? You were at university with him."

Dangerously close to throwing up, Rachel took a sip of water. No one, apart from herself, Jed and Elwyn knew that. What was Kenton's game, digging into her past like this? Had he told anyone else what he'd discovered — Harding for example? This was explosive stuff. A word in the wrong ear and her career was over.

"There were a lot of people at uni. He may have been there, but it was years ago, and I can't remember everyone." She tried to sound casual, but her voice came out strained.

"You were lovers."

Rachel stifled a gasp. This was going from bad to worse. "I was eighteen, I had lots of boyfriends."

198

"You see, Rachel, this gives us a problem. I had a close look at the Brough case notes. McAteer played an important part in resolving that investigation, plus he saved your daughter's life."

"Chance," she said tightly. "Nothing more."

Ignoring her comment, he said, "Naturally, I am coming to some disturbing conclusions."

This was the thing she'd been trying to avoid all her working life. He knew, but how much? Kenton had stopped short of actually asking if Jed was Mia's father. If he did, dare she lie?

Rachel took a deep breath. "What do you want exactly, Kenton? My job? To ruin my reputation — such as it is?"

"No, Rachel. I simply want the truth about you and McAteer. Lives may depend on it."

He was talking about the trafficked girls. Had to be. Jed was heavily involved. He might even be the head man they'd been chasing after. If she wanted to stop the suffering, she would have to be honest with Kenton.

"You're right, I did know Jed years ago," she admitted. "I can't change that. But he hasn't been part of my life since. I owe him nothing, apart from what he did for Mia, and we do not see each other. The other night was work related, to do with the current case in fact. I wanted a closer look at that apartment block."

Kenton leaned forward. "Look, Rachel, I've been on McAteer's tail for over a year. At the start, I was working on a tipoff from a reliable source of mine. Since then, me and my team have painstakingly collected all the evidence that will help to nail him. What I have learned from Leonora Blake completes the process. My reluctance to include you in the case is purely because of your relationship with McAteer. I daren't risk anything filtering back to him. Otherwise I'd have welcomed your input like a shot."

"You thought I would pass information on to him?"

"Perhaps unknowingly. I only know what I've heard or read about you, Rachel. It all looks good on paper, but I couldn't get away from the fact that you were close to the man. You have history, and you owe him for saving your daughter."

Rachel looked him in the eye. "That's not how I work. The second I discovered what McAteer was like, I dumped him. He is in my past, and that's where he's stayed. DCI Kenton, it was all many years ago. I know there can never be anything between us. And I certainly would never give him information about any of our cases. The problem is, he lives and works in Manchester, so our paths have crossed in the course of my work. I can't help that."

Rachel waited. She couldn't tell if Kenton was satisfied with that or not. She didn't know him, and couldn't second guess what his reaction might be. "What now? Do you want me to resign? Tell Harding what I've told you?"

"No. You're too good a detective. The force needs you. And I don't snitch to senior officers." He smiled. "You've been honest with me because of the case, and I appreciate that. There's no need for anyone to know what we've just spoken about."

"In that case, I'll carry on with our investigations into the murders of Agnes Moore and Jess. We have moved the case forward in the past few hours. Ruby, the missing girl, is in hospital and we're keeping close watch. You'll want to interview her, I imagine?"

He nodded. "With regard to your case, we have a lot of background information on the Blakes and Danulescu, but there is no mention of your Agnes anywhere in all the reams of paperwork. The girl called Jess may have been one of the girls working the club."

"That helps to rule out a theory, if nothing else. Go easy on Ruby, she's delicate." Rachel paused. "There's another party set for tonight at that apartment block. It should be an opportunity to collar Nicu Bogdan."

"In that case, we'll join you."

"No problem." Rachel smiled. "Since we're being so frank with each other . . . you are keeping an eye on McAteer?

200

He's clearly your prime suspect. If he gets wind of it, he'll disappear."

"Last I checked, he was in his office in Castlefields. I've got round-the-clock surveillance on him."

CHAPTER THIRTY-FOUR

The bell sounded for the end of the school day. He waited for the two teenage girls to come out and followed them as they ambled across Poynton Park, finally separating by the lake. This was his chance. Before he left the country, Jed McAteer wanted to see Mia, to say goodbye to his daughter of course, but also to find out what she knew about him.

"Mia!" He called out. "Wait up."

A little surprised at his sudden appearance, she greeted him with a big smile. "Uncle Jed! What're you doing here? You should have rung — we could have arranged something."

"Sorry to collar you like this, but it's all a bit last minute. I wanted a word because I'm going away for a while." He pointed to a vacant bench. "Want to sit down?"

"I've thought about you often. You saved my life. I still don't understand what happened. I asked Mum, but she won't talk about it."

McAteer laughed. "It's her job, she's probably not allowed to."

"She said I wasn't to see or talk to you anymore. I don't understand why. After what happened, you should be one of our best friends."

"Bad memories, perhaps," he said. "She was out of her mind with worry that day. Seeing me probably brings it all back."

"Why are you going away? Is it a holiday?"

"No, it's business, and I won't be back for quite a while."

"When I first saw you, I thought you were Mum's new boyfriend." Mia laughed. "She could do with one, Meggy reckons. Don't you fancy her?"

"I knew your mum a long time ago when we were much younger. We used to be close, but people change when they grow up. We are both different people now. It just wouldn't work."

Mia wouldn't understand, of course, not without knowing the background.

"Can I tell Mum we met?"

"Yes, and I want you to give her a message, but don't be surprised if she gets angry. For lots of reasons, your mum doesn't like me much."

"Even though you saved my life? It seems odd to me."

He shrugged. "It's just how your mum is. Anyway, I'd like to contact you from time to time, see how you're doing. Would you be okay with that?"

He could see her mulling this over. She probably thought he was a weird old man. He wanted to tell her the truth about their relationship, that he was actually her father. But not at this stage in her life. If her mother had anything about her, she'd tell Mia herself further down the line. If and when that happened, it would make the whole thing easier if they were still in touch.

"Are you really a relative — my uncle, like you said?"

"Yes, I am related to you, Mia. Though your mum will argue the point if you ask her."

After a few moments' thought, she said. "You could friend me on Facebook. That way we could stay in touch."

"I don't usually do social media, but I'll make an exception for you. But I won't be Jed, I'll be *Jenny*. That way we don't upset your mum."

She nodded. "Sounds like a plan. If you go somewhere nice, you can post photos. What d'you want me to tell her?"

"That I've been set up. I don't know who by yet, but it's a senior detective. And tell her not to trust the Salford DCI. She'll know what I mean."

Mia nodded.

It was nearly time to go. McAteer had no idea when he'd see his daughter again. By then, she could well be an adult. He took her hand. "Look after yourself, Mia. Before I go, I've got something for you." Reaching into his pocket, he took out a necklace, a gold locket encrusted with diamonds.

Mia turned it over in her hand. "These are real diamonds, aren't they? No, I can't take this." She handed it back.

"But you must. I want you to have it. It belonged to my mother, and I have no one else to give it to."

"Well, if you're sure . . ."

McAteer got to his feet. "Do as your mum tells you. Despite what you might think, she does know best."

"Keep in touch, and let me know when you're coming back."

McAteer bent down and kissed her cheek. He wished with all his heart that things were different. He longed to be a proper father to her, but Rachel wasn't ready for that.

"Take care, Mia. Be good."

They walked off in opposite directions, Mia towards her home and McAteer to his car. He was grateful for the time with Mia. He'd been lucky to get out of his office without being seen by Kenton's people. He needed to hurry. There was a private jet waiting for him at an airfield on the east coast. By the end of the day, he would be out of the country.

CHAPTER THIRTY-FIVE

"The arrest of Nicu Bogdan will be a joint effort between us and Kenton's people," Rachel told the team. She saw Elwyn's look of puzzled surprise. She'd have a word later. "In the interest of solving this case, we've called a truce. Kenton has finally agreed to share what he knows, and in return, we include him." That might satisfy the others, but Elwyn would want to know what had brought about this sudden change of heart.

"Are we to assume that Bogdan is the head man?" Jonny asked.

Rachel couldn't hide it any longer. She'd have to tell them. Kenton's people would know the truth anyway.

"No. DCI Kenton has evidence that the person organising the current spate of people trafficking in Manchester is Jed McAteer."

There was a silence. Rachel could only guess at what was going on in Elwyn's head.

"A nationwide call has gone out for his arrest," she continued. "Up until half an hour ago, DCI Kenton thought McAteer was in his office in the city. But that wasn't the case. I've just learned that he has in fact been missing since ten this morning. He could be anywhere by now."

"He knows we're onto him then?" Jonny said. "Did the new evidence come from Leonora Blake?"

"Yes, as well as other intelligence Kenton has gathered. He has been working on the trafficking racket for a year or more. When he got wind of McAteer's involvement, he had him watched. All was fine until earlier today, when he gave them the slip."

"And just when Kenton's getting somewhere, we blunder in," Elwyn commented. "I'm not surprised he didn't take to us."

Rachel smiled. "We're on the right footing now. We move forward together, arrest Bogdan and get a statement. From our point of view, we are interested in what he can tell us about Agnes. Did he know her, or visit the health centre, for example? We might have helped crack the trafficking case but we're no further forward with our own."

"Akerman told us that Agnes went to that club and complained on behalf of the girls. Danulescu wouldn't have liked that, or Leonora. Perhaps her death was down to them after all," Elwyn said.

Rachel shrugged. "It's a neat fix. But I don't think that's how it was. The method strongly suggests that Agnes and Jess were both killed by a different person. We get Nicu Bogdan and we do our best to find out."

"Ruby knows more than she's told us," Elwyn said. "Once she knows that Nicu is in custody and no longer a threat, she'll be more likely to talk to us. I reckon she's our best bet."

"I just hope someone talks to us, Elwyn. These two murders are turning out to be the most difficult cases I've ever had to solve. There is little in the way of meaningful forensics, no witnesses and no motive that we can find."

No motive. The words struck a chord. That was wrong. There had to be one. But whatever it was, it had nothing to do with the trafficking. Agnes helped those girls because they went to her in trouble. What did she get in return? And why keep their care under the radar? She'd delivered at least one infant without the knowledge of the midwifery team or the doctor. Roxanne Buckley said it was because she feared being discovered, but would Agnes really risk her career because a young girl was afraid? Rachel decided to have another word with Roxanne as soon as possible.

* * *

The plain clothes and uniformed officers were all positioned inside the apartment in good time. To give it some authenticity, a handful of young officers were hanging around in the corridor, posing as punters. Seven p.m. came and went but there was no sign of Nicu. Shannon had said he always turned up with the key, and then came later to collect. What had gone wrong? Had someone told him?

"It's the waiting that does my head in," Rachel whispered to Elwyn. "Where the hell is he?"

"Anything could have happened. Chances are he's heard about Leonora and McAteer and decided to do one himself."

"Let's hope you're wrong. Leonora's locked up and Jed's probably skipped the country by now."

Suddenly they heard a cheer from the corridor outside the apartment. They were on. A key in the lock, followed by a voice with a foreign accent warning the pretend punters to hang on.

A flurry of activity ensued. Nicu Bogdan had come alone and was quickly arrested. Heavily outnumbered, he didn't put up much of a fight.

"I'm taking him to Salford," Kenton said, appearing at the apartment door. "We'll do the interview tomorrow — say ten in the morning?"

"Things have changed between us, haven't they?" Elwyn whispered. "You still haven't told me what happened."

"For the last year, he's been delving into Jed's businesses as well as his background. In among it all, he came across my name, and that's why he was reluctant to let us in. We had a talk, and I convinced him that I can be trusted."

"And he accepted that at face value?"

Rachel gave him a long, hard look. "Well, I can be trusted, absolutely. This is my job. I wouldn't risk that for Jed."

"I know that, but how did you convince him? He seems like the sceptical type to me."

"I simply told him the truth. He knew most of it anyway."

"That's you, me, McAteer and now Kenton who know about it."

Rachel nodded. "That's about the size of it."

"And that doesn't bother you?"

"What can I do, Elwyn? He's promised it will go no further. I have no alternative but to trust him."

"I hope you're right."

CHAPTER THIRTY-SIX

Day Seven

The following morning Rachel left home and drove straight to Salford police station. Kenton was waiting for her in his office.

"He's a cool one alright. So far, he hasn't said a word. We've arranged a duty solicitor, and they're having a chat at the moment."

"What are you hoping Nicu will tell you?" Rachel asked.

"We've got a lot from Leonora Blake. She's told us about the routes and the contacts they use abroad. I'm hopeful that Nicu will fill in a few gaps nearer to home, like the clubs and so on that take the girls here in this country. That way we stand a chance of rescuing some of them."

"What if he won't talk?" Rachel asked.

"Then we'll throw the book at him and he'll go down for a long time. In McAteer's absence, he could find himself being charged with the lot."

Rachel remembered the interview with Leonora Blake. "Will you offer him a deal?"

"No. He will talk and suffer the consequences. Do you think he can help with your cases?" Kenton asked.

"I've been thinking about that and I'm not sure. He may have known both Agnes Moore and Jess, but I doubt he killed them. I need another word with Ruby and then I'll have a better picture."

"Okay, let's get started. Let's see what the young man will tell us."

Kenton led the way to the interview room, where Nicu Bogdan sat, slumped and sullen, next to his solicitor.

"I am innocent. I don't know what I'm doing here," he said on seeing the detectives.

Kenton and Rachel sat down opposite the accused man and his solicitor. Introductions dispensed with, Kenton got straight to it. "McAteer has fled the country and left you to take the rap." He gave a rare smile. "What d'you think about that then? Not fair, is it?"

Nicu looked at Rachel. "Is that right?"

"I'm afraid it is. You are in a lot of trouble. My advice is to tell us what you know and hope it will help you later on."

He was silent for a moment. "I didn't kill anybody."

"But people have been killed, Nicu," Rachel told him. "Danulescu and Blake were shot by a sniper. Do you know anything about that?"

He shook his head. "Mac will have hired someone for the job. Nothing to do with me."

"Tell me about Ruby Wood," Rachel asked. "You've spent a lot of time and energy over the last few days trying to find her. Why's that?"

"Mac wanted her silenced," he said. "She knew his name. A loose word reaching the wrong ear and the game was up."

"What about a woman called Agnes Moore? Did you know her?"

"Oh her," he said, "that interfering woman from the clinic. She tried to take the girls away. Tempted them with the promise of money and freedom."

"Where was the money coming from?" Rachel asked.

"Some scam she was running."

Was Nicu telling the truth? There had to be a reason why Agnes was murdered, and Rachel was convinced it had nothing to do with the club. What, then, was the scam?

"Do you know anything about this scam?" she said.

"Ruby wouldn't say."

* * *

After more questions, Kenton gave Nicu a break. Rachel decided to leave him to it and make her way to the hospital. Her best bet was Ruby. With luck, her health would have improved and she'd be up to talking.

"Any more trouble?" Rachel asked the officers on guard.

"No, ma'am, though I have an idea she wants out. Didn't like it much when I wouldn't let her go downstairs to the shop."

Rachel went into the room. "So, you want to leave us, Ruby. Speak to me and I'll arrange something for you."

Ruby looked at her suspiciously. "What sort of something?"

"A place to stay where you'll be safe. But you must help me first."

Ruby gave a brief nod.

"Mac has left the country and Leonora is in custody. So is Nicu. There's no need for you to be scared anymore." Rachel let this sink in before she went on. "I want you to tell me about Agnes Moore. That day you were looking for her, how was she going to help you, Ruby?"

"I wanted her to find me somewhere to stay. I was trying to get away from Nicu."

Rachel nodded. "If Agnes had still been alive, she would have kept you safe, I'm sure."

"You know nothing!" Ruby retorted. "Agnes only helped if there was a profit in it for her."

"I don't understand. What profit would she make out of you, Ruby?"

"I was going to tell her I was pregnant again."

211

What did she mean? "I know she helped pregnant girls. She was a nurse, that's understandable. But that's more likely to cost her than bring her a profit."

Ruby met Rachel's eyes and held her gaze. "You won't like it. One of the other girls at the club said it was horrific."

"Just tell me, Ruby."

"It was the babies. Agnes sold them and gave the girls a cut. Go to her pregnant, and she'd help you out."

"You're telling me that Agnes was selling babies?" Rachel couldn't believe what she'd just heard. It made no sense. That wasn't the impression she'd got of Agnes at all. But if it was true, how had she got away with it?

Ruby shrugged. "You sound shocked. A lot of the girls working in the club got pregnant, call it a hazard of the job. They gave us the pill but sometimes it didn't suit, or we'd forget to take it. Leo didn't give a toss, said it was our problem and to get it sorted. A lot of the girls went to Agnes for that. She might have been a grasping old witch, but she offered us a way out. For a fee she'd terminate the pregnancy, and for a few she offered an alternative. She'd provide a safe place to stay away from the club to see out the pregnancy. She said that the babies would go to good homes and we'd get paid. Agnes told us that there were couples out there desperate to have children. She promised that no one would find out. Who'd give a toss about us in any case?"

"How many girls were involved?" Rachel asked.

Ruby shook her head. "I've no idea about the numbers, but there was a fair few over time."

"Did the girls benefit?"

"Not really. They got a few hundred but no more than that."

"Do you remember a girl called Jess?" Rachel asked.

Ruby nodded. "She had a little boy, but then she got ill. She kept going to Agnes for treatment, causing trouble. I don't know what happened, but suddenly she wasn't around anymore."

"Jess was killed, murdered. Do you know if Agnes was responsible?" Rachel asked.

"Agnes helped us because of the money. Each baby sold for thousands. She was hard, but she wasn't a killer."

"Oh, Ruby, why didn't you tell someone about this? We could have stepped in, put a stop to it."

"I was too busy trying to stay alive. I got pregnant three months ago. I went to Agnes and she offered me the same deal. I even stayed at her flat for a while. But I lost the baby, and after that Agnes didn't want to know. I was so desperate to leave that club I pretended to be pregnant again and went back to Agnes."

"Do you know if anyone was helping Agnes?" Rachel asked.

"I never met anyone else, but there must have been. Agnes couldn't have done it all on her own."

Ruby had been through a lot in her short life. She was so young and had no one to look out for her. "You need help, Ruby, time to recover and adjust. I'll arrange for social services to come and see you. First off, you need a place to live. You can't go back on the streets." Rachel gave her a stern look. "Run away, and I'll haul you back myself. You stay here and accept the help you're offered."

Rachel felt utterly drained. What the girl had told her was truly awful. Infants sold, their mothers fobbed off and left to cope. She doubted they'd ever be able to trace them all.

Ruby was right about Agnes needing help. The woman had been holding down a full-time job, and she'd seen to the girls in her spare time. There had to be someone else involved. But who had killed her? A disgruntled customer, one of the girls, or her accomplice?

Rachel rang Jude Glover on her way to the car park. She needed the forensic results from those flakes of skin Jude had found on Agnes's clothing.

"Jude, we're desperate. We've got no one in the frame for Agnes or Jess. How is it going with the DNA from those skin flakes you found?"

"It's slow, Rachel. I can't promise anything soon. It might be an idea to ask at the health centre for a list of patients with the condition. Psoriasis isn't particularly common."

She was right, but that would require a warrant. Lorraine Hughes wasn't going to divulge such information without a fight. "Thanks, Jude."

CHAPTER THIRTY-SEVEN

Rachel returned to the station in a foul mood. She'd been up for hours and felt as if she'd already put in a full day's work.

"I've just had a harrowing conversation with Ruby," she told Elwyn. Making a reviving pot of coffee, she related the sordid details. "I can't imagine what it must be like to carry a child for months and then give it up. Agnes helped them, but that was simply so she could take full advantage of those vulnerable girls. Why did none of them complain, Elwyn? Why didn't they come to us for help?"

"They didn't have much choice. As Ruby said, pregnant girls disappeared from the club. Agnes was the only alternative."

Rachel took out her mobile. "I went to Salford first thing, and then to the hospital. I haven't even spoken to my kids this morning. Mia was asleep when I got in last night and Meggy was out. I'm a crap mother, Elwyn. I need to give my priorities a good looking at." Neither girl picked up. "They have their faces permanently stuck in these bloody things, but when I ring . . ."

"They'll be busy, and you're a fine mother. You're upset, that's all. Who wouldn't be? Want me to relay this to the team?" Elwyn said.

"Please. I need to think, look at what we've got with fresh eyes. We've wasted a lot of time searching in the wrong place for the wrong motive."

There was a knock on her door.

"You're a hard one to pin down," Stuart Knight began. "I've got some info you should know about. It's that young couple who came in with a complaint. I took the details but after seeing the notes on your incident board, I thought you should take a look."

That scam Jonny had mentioned. "Oh? Why do I need to know about it?"

"This couple, they knew Agnes Moore for a start."

Rachel sat up. "Did you take a statement?"

He nodded. "It's not particularly detailed. Only that they'd given Agnes Moore a large amount of money and got nothing in return. Whatever she was supposed to sell them was not forthcoming."

Rachel knew very well what it was. "Where do I find this couple?"

Knight passed her the file. "Their address is in there. They were very cut up about it. They'd parted with their life savings, apparently."

Rachel's first thought was that it served them right, but she said nothing to Knight. "Thanks, I'll follow it up."

The couple, Colin and Rosemary Lovatt, lived in Collyhurst on the outskirts of Manchester. Rachel went out into the incident room. "Elwyn, we've got something. Get your coat, we're off out."

"Where're we going?"

"Collyhurst. I think we've found two of Agnes's customers. They paid over the money but never received the goods. Can you believe they were about to buy a baby and now have the cheek to consider themselves victims of a con."

Elwyn looked through the file. "Why haven't we heard of them before now?"

"Knight was investigating the complaint. He saw the stuff on our board and realised we needed to know."

"Rung your girls?"

"You drive and I'll give it another go," she said.

Mia was at school, but Rachel finally got through to Megan.

"You went off sharpish. I wanted a word," Megan said. "Me and Mia had a right set-to last night. You need to have a word with her."

"Why? What's up?"

"Belinda saw her in Poynton Park, talking to a strange man. Belinda knows everyone around here and she said he wasn't local. I asked Mia, but she clammed up and wouldn't tell me anything. And she's got an expensive-looking necklace. It's not one of yours and she won't tell me where it came from. I'm worried about her, Mum. I've no idea what she's got herself into."

As if she didn't have enough to think about. "Is Mia at school?"

"Yes. Will you be here when she gets home?"

Given the state of play with the current case, that was a big ask. "I'll do my best. Just try and keep the peace until I do get there. I'll sort it out, don't worry."

"Problem?" Elwyn asked.

"Isn't there always?" Rachel said wearily. She didn't have the energy to give him the details.

* * *

The Lovatts lived in a neat semi on a new estate in Collyhurst, on the outskirts of the city.

"The car's in the drive," Elwyn said.

"Good. Save us coming back." Rachel wasn't in the best of moods. She needed this pair's help, but what she really wanted was to throw the book at them.

They'd been seen. The detectives were only halfway up the path when a young woman opened the door.

"You're the police? I've been expecting you." She beckoned them inside. "Go straight through."

217

"You know why we're here?" Rachel began. "You made a complaint, I understand."

"I certainly did. That woman took our money and we got nothing in return. It has to be a scam. She could be doing this to lots of other couples. You need to warn people."

The cheek of the woman! Rachel could barely believe it. All that bothered her was losing the money. She seemed quite at ease with the fact that she'd handed it over for the purchase of a baby.

"You were buying a baby," Rachel said. "Did you not see anything wrong with that?"

From the astonished look on Rosemary Lovatt's face, she obviously didn't.

"No. We had a surrogate, all perfectly above board. That's what Agnes told us. She promised us that everything we were doing was lawful and that she'd helped people like us many times before."

"It wasn't lawful. The girls did not want to be pregnant but they were too far gone to do anything about it. Agnes was their last resort. She took the infants and sold them to people like you. The girls got very little out of the deal."

Rosemary Lovatt obviously didn't believe her. "That can't be right. Agnes said the money would be used to look after the girls during the pregnancy. Our surrogate was sickly and couldn't work. The money paid her rent and expenses."

"How much did you give her?" Rachel asked.

"Twenty thousand pounds."

That was some scam Agnes had going. Rachel wondered how many times she'd done this. "Some of the girls Agnes used were living on the streets. At least one is dead — murdered. There is no way that was legal!" Rachel was losing it.

Elwyn cleared his throat. "Shall we take a break?"

"I'm fine," Rachel said impatiently. "Who else did you meet, apart from Agnes?"

"No one."

"Not even your so-called surrogate? Didn't you think that odd?"

"Agnes said she'd arrange it, but then she disappeared."

Rachel shook her head. "Agnes was murdered. It seems that someone didn't think very much of her business."

"You can't believe me and my husband had anything to do with that! We're angry, yes. We've lost a lot of money, but we'd never harm anyone."

"Agnes and a young girl have lost their lives," Rachel said. "Our priority is to find their killer. Did you try to phone Agnes?"

"Lots of times. I kept asking how things were going, if the baby was doing alright. I was worried because the surrogate wasn't well."

"You rang her mobile?"

"Usually, and once or twice I rang her home."

"We'll check your phone data," Rachel said.

"Check what you like, we've nothing to hide."

CHAPTER THIRTY-EIGHT

On their way back to the station, Rachel went over her notes. "Amy looked at Agnes's bank records when she was doing the background search. How come there was no sign of the money? The woman must have made a fortune these last few years."

"Maybe she hid it," Elwyn suggested.

"I don't think so. She had to have had an accomplice, Elwyn. They have the money and are possibly our killer."

"You don't suspect the Lovatts?" he asked.

"Heavens, no. That woman didn't even realise that what they did was wrong. She truly believed that Agnes had arranged a surrogate and the money was for expenses."

"Back to square one it is then," Elwyn said.

Rachel groaned, but it looked as if they had no choice. "We look at everyone Agnes was involved with, particularly at work. It would make sense if she looked for help from someone who knew the ropes and could help with the girls. Jude has suggested we ask about patients with psoriasis. It'll be quicker than waiting for the results from the lab."

"Who do we haul in first?"

"Lorraine Hughes," Rachel said. "I always thought she was a bit dubious. What about you?"

Elwyn shook his head. "It's a long shot, Rachel. Agnes's accomplice could be anyone, and they might not even be her killer. What we're doing now is putting names in a bag, shaking it, and then pulling them out in turn."

"Nonetheless, she'll do for starters. We'll bring the woman in and interview her properly."

"She won't like it."

But Rachel was intent on her notes.

* * *

Having refused a solicitor, Lorraine Hughes sat with Rachel and Elwyn in a soft interview room.

"We suspect that Agnes had an accomplice. Do you have any idea who that might have been?" Rachel asked.

"Accomplice in what? I don't even know what she's supposed to have done," Lorraine said. "Look, we've been through all this. Agnes was a colleague. I liked her. I certainly didn't kill her."

"We believe that the reason Agnes was killed had something to do with those girls that used to come to the health centre. You weren't the least bit suspicious of her? You didn't wonder why she helped them?"

Lorraine was adamant. "She was a good woman. Misguided perhaps, but she believed in what she was doing. I admired Agnes for that. She was a far better person than I could ever be. She worked unceasingly for those girls."

There was no doubting it. Lorraine Hughes meant every word of what she was saying. She seemed to believe Agnes was a good person, and had no inkling of the truth.

Rachel smiled at her. "Thanks for coming in. We won't need to interview you again. We will need to visit the surgery, though. We are trying to find someone Agnes knew who suffered with the skin condition psoriasis."

"Her sister," Lorraine Hughes said at once. "Covered in it when she gets stressed. Terrible condition. Gives her no peace." She put a hand to her mouth. "Oh dear, I shouldn't have told you that. But Anthea isn't one of our patients, so I've not breached confidentiality."

Rachel was surprised. "Anthea Moore has psoriasis?"

"I just said so. You've met her. I'm surprised you didn't notice. She has it all up her arms. It's what makes her so bad tempered. It got Agnes down every bit as much as Anthea herself. It was why she moved out."

"You can go now, Lorraine, and thank you, you've been a great help."

"The sister," Elwyn said as soon as the door closed behind her. "That's a surprise."

"I'll get a warrant. Stella can trawl through her finances. We might just have cracked it, Elwyn."

* * *

Rachel and Elwyn pulled up outside the house in Audenshaw. Anthea Moore was off work on compassionate leave, so they expected her to be at home.

"The warrant isn't through yet," Rachel said, "so we'll take it slow. Once it is, we'll get access to her bank accounts and do a full search of the house. That gun was never found, so she could have brought it back here.

A tearful Anthea answered the door.

"I'm having a moment," she said. "It's just beginning to hit me that I'll never see Agnes again."

Rachel got straight to the point. "Can you tell us where you were the night your sister was killed?" The tears, the pretence — because that's what it was, Rachel was certain — was getting on her nerves.

"I . . . I was here."

"Can anyone vouch for that? Give you an alibi?" Elwyn asked.

Anthea's expression quickly changed to one of annoyance. "What is this? You surely don't imagine that I had anything to do with Agnes's death?"

"Did you know what she was up to? The runaway girls and the baby scam?" asked Elwyn.

"I don't have a clue what you're on about." Anthea started to scratch at her arm.

"Giving you a hard time, is it? You won't know, but we found flakes of skin on Agnes's clothing. How did that happen, d'you think?" Rachel said.

"I know what you're trying to do. You think you can pin this on me. There'll be a logical explanation. I didn't kill Agnes, and you can't prove that I did. How dare you come here and make these accusations!"

"We'll have a warrant very soon. Then we'll search your house and go through your bank accounts. If we find money and any incriminating items, you'll go down for a long time. Better you speak to us, give us your version of events," Elwyn said.

Anthea looked around her. She seemed to be trying to work out which way to turn.

"I'm saying nothing. Why should I make your job any easier? You want to charge me, get the evidence."

Rachel went out into the hall and rang the incident room. Jonny Farrell answered. "The warrant. Have we got it yet?"

"Yes, ma'am. Amy's on her way over with it now and I've rung Dr Glover. I'm looking at her bank accounts right now. She has quite a tidy sum stashed away."

That would do for a start. Back in the sitting room, Anthea perched on the edge of the sofa. "You're wasting your time. We had our differences, but I would never harm Agnes."

"We're taking you to the station, Anthea. My colleagues have a warrant and they'll soon be here to start the search."

"The station? What on earth for? What do you imagine I've got to tell you?"

"You can try the truth," Elwyn said.

Anthea's continued denials bothered Rachel. Ideally, they would like to find the gun that had been used to kill both Agnes and Jess. If it wasn't here, and she wouldn't talk, they might have a hard time convincing the CPS that they had a case. Flakes of skin were one thing, but Agnes came to this house regularly, so any solicitor worth his salt could explain that away easily.

"Keep an eye on her, Elwyn. I'm going for a wander round the back."

Rachel had no idea what she'd find. The rear garden was small and backed onto a parking area for the residents. She saw a lawn, a flower border and a small shed. Plenty of places to hide a gun. Things would be so much simpler if Anthea simply told them the truth.

Rachel was just about to go back inside when she spotted it. Parked against Anthea's rear wall was a white van. She smiled and hurried back inside.

"Who owns the white van, Anthea? The one parked against your wall?"

"I don't know," she said sullenly.

Rachel rang Jude and asked her to include the van when she did her search. She also rang Stella and asked her to find the registered owner.

A police car arrived to take Anthea Moore away, while Rachel and Elwyn waited at the house for Jude and her people.

Not long after Anthea had left, Stella rang back. "It's registered to a Barry Wallwork. He lives next door to Anthea."

Rachel beckoned to Elwyn "We need a word with the neighbour."

Wallwork was a self-employed odd-job man. He invited the pair in and happily handed over the van keys when they asked for them.

"It won't go," he said. "That's why I'm not working. Anthea borrowed it last week, and since then I can't get it into gear. She's refusing to admit she did any damage, but it was fine before she went off with it."

"D'you know what she wanted it for?" Rachel asked.

"No, but it came back in a right state. Covered in mud it was."

"Can I ask what you currently have in the van," Elwyn said.

"I've been clearing an attic, removing the insulation and replacing it with new stuff. Jobs like that are easy money, but now I'll have to spend what I earned to get the van fixed." Wallwork shook his head.

"Some of our colleagues will be here soon. They'll want to look at your van and take some samples. They do have a warrant," Rachel said.

"They can do what they want." He paused. "Bloody woman."

CHAPTER THIRTY-NINE

Anthea Moore sat quietly with her solicitor in the interview room.

"You know why we're here," Rachel said. "Tell us what happened the night Agnes died."

"I've already told you I had nothing to do with it, and I've nothing more to add."

"Anthea, we found the gun in your shed. We know you used your neighbour's van to transport Agnes to that building site. Why not simply tell us the truth?"

She gazed back at them, her eyes defiant. "You can't prove anything. I've never touched that gun. It belonged to our father. Damn thing scares me to death."

"We have a forensic team working on evidence we've gathered. They'll find your fingerprints and other DNA evidence to prove you killed your sister. It'll go easier for you in court if you're straight with us."

"You don't understand what it was like. Agnes was not the saint everyone said, you know. She could be wicked. People thought I was the hard one, but truly, Agnes was a force to be reckoned with."

"Make a statement, Anthea. Tell us what happened to both Agnes and the girl, Jess Darwin."

"No!"

* * *

Later that day, the team gathered to discuss what they had.

"Despite growing evidence of her guilt, Anthea Moore is still refusing to admit that she killed Agnes or Jess," Rachel told them. "And believe me, we've really tried to prise the truth out of her. Jude Glover and her team have found fibre-glass in the van from rolls of insulation belonging to the owner, and hopefully tests will prove it was the same as that on Agnes's clothing. The gun was found in the garden shed, locked in a cupboard along with Agnes's shoes. God knows what Anthea wanted them for. They're doing tests on the gun to see if it's the murder weapon, and to check if it has Anthea's prints on it."

"Can we prove that Anthea was in on the baby thing with Agnes?" Jonny asked.

"There's a small fortune in her bank account and she can't explain how it got there. She keeps bleating on about saving up, but she couldn't save that much in several life-times. There was no inheritance to account for it either."

"Have we got enough to make a case, ma'am?" Amy asked.

"Yes, Amy. Prior to this meeting, I had a word with Harding, and he reckons we're on. Anthea wears a ring, a big hunk of fake emerald. It has a sharp edge. Jude is checking it against a cut on Agnes's cheek. She expects to find traces of Anthea's blood. That will put Anthea firmly at the scene of the murder."

"Ma'am." It was the custody sergeant. "The prisoner, Anthea Moore has asked to see you."

"Break through, d'you think? Is she about to come clean then?" Jonny asked.

"I certainly hope so." Rachel took hold of the paperwork, gestured for Elwyn to join her and made for the interview room. "Room three," she told the sergeant.

Anthea's face was tear-stained. "I'm sorry," she said. "I need to tell you the truth, make a clean break. It really wasn't my fault, Agnes made me so angry at times. I swear she cared more about those girls than me. She spent a fortune on them, even helped one furnish her house."

Rachel presumed that was Roxanne Buckley. "Tell us what happened the night Agnes died," she said.

"We argued, no it was worse than that, we came to blows. I hit her, caught her face with my ring. Agnes wanted out. She told me she'd had enough. I said no, we had a good thing going. I have four couples on the books waiting for babies, that's a lot of money. But Agnes wasn't interested. That girl, Jess, had been the final straw. After she died, Agnes couldn't think straight. I tried to explain that I had no choice, that I was doing us a favour. Jess threatened us with the law, so she had to die. It was either her or us. Agnes wanted to know what had happened. I explained that me and the girl had argued and how she'd refused to see reason, but Agnes still wasn't happy. I took her to that place, the building site and showed her where the girl was. I thought it would make her understand. But I've never seen Agnes so angry, she was like a mad woman. I had to stop her."

"You shot her with your father's gun?" Rachel asked.

"Agnes refused to see it from my point of view. I had no choice."

* * *

Rachel and Elwyn returned to the incident room. "We've got a full confession." Rachel said. But she could only manage a half-hearted smile. It had been a long hard slog, and there were still matters outstanding. Knowing how Agnes and Jess had met their deaths was one thing but she'd no idea what had happened to Leonora Blake. Kenton would say nothing other than it was over. The case might be closed, but it still irked her. More troubling than anything else was the possibility that Jed had been involved in a people-trafficking operation.

"Time to call it a day," she told the team. "Well done, everyone."

"You look done in," Elwyn said "Fancy a drink? The team are meeting in the pub."

"Thanks, but no. I've got some sort of drama kicking off at home, so I'd better get going."

He stared at her. "You're not happy, are you? What is it?"

"Everything fits into place except the bit about Jed." She saw Elwyn's look of scepticism. "Yes, he's a crook, and I know he's done all sorts in his time. I'm under no illusions about what he's capable of, but he's never stooped this low. People trafficking, Elwyn! That just isn't Jed. He can't possibly be the ring's head man."

Elwyn still looked doubtful. "Kenton reckons he's done his research. He's got evidence, he says. He has an excellent clear-up rate and is tipped for high office. I wouldn't go out of my way to cross him, Rachel. You don't want Kenton as an enemy."

"He's got whatever lies Leonora Blake told him. Everyone else is dead."

"The name *Mac* on Danulescu's phone, the one Ruby saw. What about that?" Elwyn said.

"That means nothing, and you know it. The entire Greater Manchester underworld knows him as Mac. He's made enough enemies in his time. This could be payback."

"Let it drop, Rachel. It'll do you no good."

The notion that McAteer had somehow been set up persisted. But she was wasting her time trying to convince

Elwyn. For now, she'd take his advice, but Rachel promised herself that sometime in the future, she would look at the evidence again, even if it meant cultivating Kenton's friendship.

EPILOGUE

It was over. Anthea Moore had been charged with the murder of her sister Agnes and Jess Darwin. Rachel was on her way home to tackle the domestic crisis that had been unfolding all day while she was busy on the case. All she knew was what she could glean from her daughters' cryptic texts. Mia and Megan had had another blazing row after school. Mia was still refusing to tell Megan who she'd been talking to in the park, so now Alan was involved.

"It was a man, Mum. How many times have we told her? After what happened to her that time, you'd think she'd be more careful."

"Fair comment, but Mia is an outgoing girl. Perhaps this man's the parent of a schoolmate of hers," Rachel suggested without much hope.

"He wasn't anyone dangerous," Mia insisted, "and you know him, Mum."

"Then tell us, idiot," Megan said, pushing her onto the sofa.

"I do?" Rachel said. And then it dawned on her. "Uncle Jed?"

Mia nodded.

"There you are then." Rachel spoke matter-of-factly, but the nerves were at it again. "He saved her life, so he's hardly likely to do her harm, is he?"

"So why didn't the stupid kid just tell us? Oh, I give up!" Megan stormed off to her room.

"I take it I'm not needed anymore?" Alan said.

Rachel smiled at him. "I'll sort them from here."

"Thanks. Me and Belinda are going out for a meal and I've got to get ready."

Get ready. He was behaving like a schoolgirl with a crush. Not that Rachel was bothered. She was perfectly happy to have him out of the way.

Finally, she and Mia were alone. "Jed gave you something, Megan said."

Mia held up the locket. "He said it was his mother's. I did say I couldn't take it, but he wasn't having any."

Rachel smiled. "It's beautiful. Keep it safe, and don't let your sister borrow it."

"I'm not in trouble then?" Mia asked.

"No. Jed isn't a secret, not really. He was involved in a case of mine, that's all. And he did save your life. We're very grateful to him for that."

"You knew him years ago when you were young. He told me." Mia looked almost accusing.

But Rachel wasn't up to explanations. "Did he say where he was going?"

"Just away. And for a while. He wanted me to tell you something. Doesn't make much sense to me, but then the stuff you adults say never does."

"Go on then, what was it?"

"He said to tell you that he's been set up and by a high-ranking policeman."

Mia's attention was already on her mobile, looking at the image of Ella, her best friend, and she went off to her room to chat.

Set up? Was that true? Rachel wanted to believe it was so. All her instincts told her that Jed wasn't a trafficker. But if she was right, who had set him up and why?

Whatever the truth, it would have to wait. Rachel was exhausted and there was no evidence to support such an outlandish theory. Mark Kenton might be CID's latest superstar, but this time he hadn't got the result he wanted. In the end, Jed McAteer had outwitted him. Rachel smiled to herself.

THE END

ALSO BY HELEN H. DURRANT

THE DETECTIVE RACHEL KING BOOKS
Book 1: *Next Victim*
Book 2: *Two Victims*
Book 3: *Wrong Victim*
Book 4: *Forgotten Victim*

THE DCI GRECO BOOKS
Book 1: *Dark Murder*
Book 2: *Dark Houses*
Book 3: *Dark Trade*
Book 4: *Dark Angel*

THE CALLADINE & BAYLISS MYSTERY SERIES
Book 1: *Dead Wrong*
Book 2: *Dead Silent*
Book 3: *Dead List*
Book 4: *Dead Lost*
Book 5: *Dead & Buried*
Book 6: *Dead Nasty*
Book 7: *Dead Jealous*
Book 8: *Dead Bad*
Book 9: *Dead Guilty*
Book 10: *Dead Wicked*

MATT BRINDLE
Book 1: *His Third Victim*
Book 2: *The Other Victim*

DETECTIVES LENNOX & WILDE
Book 1: *The Guilty Man*
Book 2: *The Faceless Man*

Thank you for reading this book.

If you enjoyed it please leave feedback on Amazon or Goodreads, and if there is anything we missed or you have a question about, then please get in touch. We appreciate you choosing our book.

Founded in 2014 in Shoreditch, London, we at Joffe Books pride ourselves on our history of innovative publishing. We were thrilled to be shortlisted for Independent Publisher of the Year at the British Book Awards.

www.joffebooks.com

Join our mailing list to be the first to hear about Helen H. Durrant's next mystery, coming soon!